SEIZE THE FIRE

BY LAURA KINSALE
New York Times bestselling author

AN UNLIKELY PRINCESS SHIPWRECKED
WITH A WAR HERO WHO'S GOT HELL TO PAY

Her Serene Highness Olympia of Oriens—plump, demure, and idealistic—longs to return to her tiny, embattled land and lead her people to justice and freedom. Famous hero Captain Sheridan Drake, destitute and tormented by nightmares of the carnage he's seen, means only to rob and abandon her. What is Olympia to do with the tortured man behind the hero's façade? And how will they cope when their very survival depends on each other?

978-1-402

D0003522

MIDSUMMER MOON

BY LAURA KINSALE
New York Times bestselling author

IF HE REALLY LOVED HER,
WOULDN'T HE HELP HER REALIZE HER DREAM?

When inventor Merlin Lambourne is endangered by Napoleon's advancing forces, Lord Ransom Falconer, in service of his government, comes to her rescue and falls under the spell of her beauty and absent-minded brilliance. But he is horrified by her dream of building a flying machine—and not only because he is determined to keep her safe.

978-1-4022-1398-4 • $7.99 U.S./$8.99 CAN

"What are you doing, Ian?"

He guided a hank of hair back over her shoulder. "Bad idea, huh?"

Agree with the man, she commanded herself. *Tell him not to be foolish. Tell him that yes, absolutely, it's a bad, bad idea.* But her mouth opened, and she heard herself say softly, intimately, "You never made a move before."

"You're too important to me." He traced a line down the center of her nose, leaving a trail of longing, a sizzle of sweet heat.

And she needed to call him on his crap. "I'm too important, you just said."

"That's right. You are."

"And yet, tonight, you want to pretend that I'm not?"

His forehead crinkled with a frown. "Didn't I just say it's not wise?"

"But you're doing it anyway."

His breathing changed, his dilated pupils sharpening, a muscle twitching at his jaw. "You're right. I'm messed up tonight and not thinking clearly. You need to get up and go."

She did no such thing.

"I need you to tell me why. Why tonight, of all nights, you want to change the rules?"

"Ell..."

"Just tell me why, Ian. That's what I need to know."

THE BRAVOS OF VALENTINE BAY: They're finding love—and having babies!—in the Pacific Northwest

Dear Reader,

Here we are at book ten of the ten-book Bravos of Valentine Bay series. If this is your first visit to Valentine Bay, I want to reassure you that I always construct each story to be read as a stand-alone. You'll get all the great feels and the satisfaction at the end by reading *The Last One Home* on its own.

Finn Bravo has been missing for two decades now. He vanished at the age of eight on a family trip to Russia. His siblings in Valentine Bay, Oregon, have never stopped looking for him—and they never will, though every promising lead so far has come to a dead end. His family is determined to bring him home someday.

Ian McNeill, CEO and owner of a successful New York City toy company, has never known where he came from. Adopted from a Russian orphanage at around the age of ten, he considers himself a lucky man. The waking nightmare he survived in Siberia is behind him and he loved his now-deceased adoptive mother. The way he sees it, a wife and family of his own just aren't in the cards for him, but he's always grateful for how his life turned out.

Single mom Ella Haralson is Ian's colleague at work and also his friend. Her eleven-year-old daughter, Abby, considers Ian something of a second dad. But when buried memories from Ian's past resurface, Ella will step up for him in any way he needs her. And just maybe the two of them will discover that there's a lot more than friendship going on between them.

I hope this story grabs you from page one, holds you right through to the end and brings home to you the enduring power of friendship, love and family.

Happy reading, everyone,

Christine

The Last One Home

CHRISTINE RIMMER

HARLEQUIN

SPECIAL
EDITION

Recycling programs
for this product may
not exist in your area.

ISBN-13: 978-1-335-40483-1

The Last One Home

Copyright © 2021 by Christine Rimmer

All rights reserved. No part of this book may be used or reproduced in any manner whatsoever without written permission except in the case of brief quotations embodied in critical articles and reviews.

This is a work of fiction. Names, characters, places and incidents are either the product of the author's imagination or are used fictitiously. Any resemblance to actual persons, living or dead, businesses, companies, events or locales is entirely coincidental.

This edition published by arrangement with Harlequin Books S.A.

For questions and comments about the quality of this book, please contact us at CustomerService@Harlequin.com.

Harlequin Enterprises ULC
22 Adelaide St. West, 40th Floor
Toronto, Ontario M5H 4E3, Canada
www.Harlequin.com

Printed in U.S.A.

Christine Rimmer came to her profession the long way around. She tried everything from acting to teaching to telephone sales. Now she's finally found work that suits her perfectly. She insists she never had a problem keeping a job—she was merely gaining "life experience" for her future as a novelist. Christine lives with her family in Oregon. Visit her at christinerimmer.com.

Books by Christine Rimmer

Harlequin Special Edition

The Bravos of Valentine Bay

Almost a Bravo
Same Time, Next Christmas
Switched at Birth
A Husband She Couldn't Forget
The Right Reason to Marry
Their Secret Summer Family
Home for the Baby's Sake
A Temporary Christmas Arrangement

Montana Mavericks: What Happened to Beatrix?

In Search of the Long-Lost Maverick

Montana Mavericks: Six Brides for Six Brothers

Her Favorite Maverick

Montana Mavericks: The Lonelyhearts Ranch

A Maverick to (Re)Marry

Visit the Author Profile page
at Harlequin.com for more titles.

For MSR, always.

Chapter One

"We never see the bears, Ian. I think we should." Abby Haralson gazed up at Ian McNeill with a bright smile on her wide-eyed, lightly freckled face. The kid had been wrapping him around her pinkie finger for nine years now—ever since the age of two, when her mother, Ella, brought her to work for the first time. That day, Abby had climbed into his lap without being invited and then refused to get down.

He'd been nineteen then, working summers and part-time during the school year while he earned his degree, determined to master every job at Patch&Pebble, the toy company he would someday inherit from the woman who had saved him and claimed him as her son.

On that first day he met toddler Abby, she'd turned those big brown eyes on him, same as now. She'd smiled so sweetly—and peed on his brand-new suit.

As for the bears, no. Just no. "Not today, Abby."

"Well, Ian, then when?" She fluttered her eyelashes, her smile turning wistful. No doubt about it, Abby was destined to break a whole bunch of hearts.

"I don't know. One of these days." He and Abby had their things they did together—Yankees and Knicks games, in the good seats, down close to the action. He took her to her favorite Disney movies now and then, to see *Frozen* and *The Lion King* on Broadway, and he attended her dance recitals. A couple of times a year, on days like today when the weather was right, when he could get away and she didn't have school, they spent an afternoon in Central Park, including a visit to the zoo. Never once in all those years had they gone to see the bears.

And Ian had no intention of going to see them now.

"Ian." Abby pinched up her mouth at him. "It's like Nike. You need to just do it. You'll be surprised. It's going to be fine. Betty and Veronica are *really* friendly grizzly bears. We read about them in class.

They are *so* friendly that, for their own safety, Betty had to be removed from Montana and Veronica had to be taken out of Yellowstone—so Ian, come on. Don't you want to see the *friendly* bears?"

No, Ian did not.

But there was just something about Abby. She could make him do what she wanted him to do using only her big eyes and that angelic smile. Now, she kept both trained on him expectantly as she waited for him to say yes. He almost said it.

But bears?

Not going to happen.

Ian frankly acknowledged his fear of bears— even ones safely locked in fancy outdoor cages. Maybe someday he'd deal with that fear. Not today, though.

"What about the seals?" he suggested. "You love the seals."

Abby planted her legs apart and braced her fists on her hips, adorably adamant. "Betty and Veronica can't hurt you, Ian. They're in a special bear habitat and they can't get near the people."

"I'm aware of that."

"Ian." She pulled out all the stops, folding her arms, sticking out her chin and puffing up her chest. "You really need to face your fears."

Bemused by her absolute unwillingness to let it go, he stared down at her as she gave him a bullet-point rundown of a story she'd read during library time about a Midwestern farmer's daughter who faced her deepest fear and jumped out of a hayloft.

"How'd that work out for her?"

Abby wrinkled her freckled nose at him. "Okay, she broke her leg. But it was *character building*, and that's what matters."

Ian bit the inside of his lip to keep from grinning. Abby could be so stern and earnest. "I'm not *that* afraid of bears," he lied. "Have you forgotten? *Patch* is a bear." Patch was one of the two all-time top-selling toys manufactured by his company.

Abby scoffed. "Patch is a *stuffie*."

"And stuffed bears are my favorite kind."

"But why don't you like *real* bears?" As she asked the question, her glance shifted to the faded white scar that ran upward diagonally from his left temple, barely skirting his eye, to the center of his forehead. Once she'd compared it to Harry Potter's lightning-bolt scar, though Ian's scar was ragged, uneven and not the least photogenic.

"Abby, you already know why I avoid real bears." She'd known how he got that scar since the age of eight, when she'd coaxed him into telling her how it happened—or at least, as much as he remembered of how it happened.

"Oh, Ian…" A mournful sigh escaped her. "Betty and Veronica won't hurt you."

"Betty and Veronica are *bears*. That's all I need to know—and how about the flamingos?" he offered hopefully. "Let's head over there."

Abby slowly shook her head. "There is nothing to worry about. I *promise* you. I'll be right there with you, Ian." And she slipped her hand in his.

That did it. He couldn't deny her. Besides, her reasoning rang true; they were just bears in the zoo. Bears in a special habitat, walled off from the humans. Nice bears. Friendly ones—according to Abby, anyway. How bad could it be?

Five minutes later, Ian stood next to Abby at the shatterproof viewing screen above the grizzly habitat and stared down at the two giant bears below.

Surprisingly, nothing happened. He didn't find himself paralyzed with terror. No flashing visions assailed him. He had zero urge to run away screaming.

"See?" Abby nudged him with her elbow. He could hear the grin in her voice. "You're just fine."

"It appears so." *At least, for the moment.*

The horror might still kick in.

But he watched the bears a little longer, and still it didn't.

He heard himself chuckle. They were enormous, those two bears. And playful. They snuffled and shuffled and slid around in the water, climbing out onto the rocks, rolling in again.

As for Ian, he felt relaxed and amused, not the least panicked. He had to hand it to the kid. Turning to meet her eyes, he said, "You're right, Abby. I should have let you drag me here years ago."

"Yes, you should have." Her smile had turned smug. Abby loved being right.

He shifted his attention back through the viewing screen, smiling at his own fears just as Betty threw back her enormous furry head and let out a roar that showed way too many long, sharp teeth.

It happened right then.

Like a stop-motion movie, the images began. They flashed and vanished in front of his eyes. Strobing and pulsing, they filled his head, each more terrifying than the one before it.

They flipped by faster and faster.

He was thrown back in time, only a boy and scared out of his mind.

Shadows on snow, blood on the white. Angry growls, long, piercing claws reaching for him, sharp teeth coming at him…

His vision zeroed to a tiny circle in the center of an endless night—no stars, no moon—nothing to light the unremitting dark.

As he sank to the ground, from somewhere far away, he could hear Abby screaming. He needed to comfort her, to promise her that it was all in his mind, that everything would be all right.

But he couldn't move. He stared up at a pinprick of blue sky surrounded by darkness.

And everything went black.

Chapter Two

In the blackness, something different happened.

He was still just a kid, but not terrified, not alone. He tagged after an older boy along a snowy path. Somehow, he knew that the older boy was his brother, Matt.

Matt turned to him and ordered him to go back to the others.

His boy self insisted, "Mom said I could come with you," and he kept following, chattering away about how he thought the huskies that pulled their sled were so cool, with their weird, bright blue eyes. "I want a husky, Matt. I'm asking Mom for one when we get home."

Matt turned on him again, glaring. "Just shut up, will you, Finnegan? Just. Please. Stop. Talking."

He stared up at his brother and did what Matt said, pressing his lips together so no words could get out. Matt made a sound of disgust low in his throat, turned back around and started walking again.

*His boy self kept quiet after that. He trudged along through the snow behind his grumpy big brother, thinking that Matt was a dick and wishing he had the nerve to say the bad word out loud. He even practiced it, mouthing the accusation—*You're a dick, Matt—*but not giving it sound.*

A few minutes went by. He started to find it difficult to keep being mad at Matt. Being mad was hard, and it didn't feel good. He let his anger go and opened his mouth to say more about getting a husky when he spotted movement from the corner of his eye.

Blinking, he swung his head that way and saw it was a chipmunk, only white—a white chipmunk. "Wow," he whispered to himself. "Just, wow."

The chipmunk had pale tan stripes and a fluffy white tail. Its white fur made it difficult to spot against the snow. It got up on its rear legs, sniffed the air—and then darted off toward a tangle of bare bushes.

Fascinated, he took off in pursuit of the cute lit-tle creature, veering away from Matt to give chase as it raced across the snow—and wait.

What was that?

It sounded like crying...

The sound brought the darkness back, the snowy world zeroing down to a pinprick of bright-ness.

Ian blinked and stared up at the girl bending over him. "Abby?"

She sobbed, "Ian! Oh, Ian, I'm so, so sorry…"

His vision still blurry, his mind a gray fog, he tried to reach up, to soothe her, but his arms wouldn't move.

Someone pushed her back.

Abby disappeared from his line of sight. Now he frowned up at the tired face of a concerned-looking dark-haired woman. She wore a blue uni-form with *FDNY* over the left pocket and *EMT* above the right. He managed to form two words. "I'm fine…"

The woman shook her head and spoke to him. He heard nothing but a flood of garbled sounds until the last word. "…hospital."

"Hospital? I don't need to go to any hospital—Abby!" He called for her. Somewhere nearby, he could hear her, still crying. He struggled again to free his arms, to kick his legs, which wouldn't move, either. As he struggled, he tried to reassure her, shouting, "I'm fine, Abby! Abby, don't cry…" He looked up at the EMT and said in a pleading voice, "Really, I'm all right…" He glanced down at himself and put it together: strapped to a gurney. When had that happened?

"Ian!" Abby called from behind another blue uniform. "I'll go with you…"

Yes. If they were taking him anywhere, Abby had damn well better come, too. "Let her come in the ambulance," he said to the woman bending over him. "She's only eleven. You can't leave her here."

The woman only patted his shoulder gently and spoke in a coaxing tone. "Don't worry. You're going to be fine."

As they loaded him into the red-and-white vehicle, he kept saying, "No!" and kept calling for Abby.

Finally the woman said what he needed to hear. "She's coming. Stop struggling. She'll ride along."

And then he was in the small, enclosed space— with Abby beside him, her eyes red from crying, but her expression calm and determined. "It's okay," she promised him, patting his shoulder with one hand and holding up her jewel-bedecked pink phone with the other. "I'm here, Ian. Right here with you. I've called Mom. She's meeting us at Manhattan General…"

"Good…" Abby needed her mom, and he needed Ella, too. His longtime friend and, for the last four years, chief operating officer at Patch&Pebble, Ella had a way about her. Calm and no-nonsense, she took every crisis in stride.

Abby sniffled—but bravely. "You're going to be fine."

"Of course I am. I'm sorry I scared you."

She patted his shoulder again. "I feel so *terrible*. I shouldn't have—"

"Honey, you need to sit," the EMT cut in. Gently, she guided Abby to a bench by the doors. "Buckle up," the woman said.

Then she took Abby's place at his side.

Hours later, the doctors at Manhattan General had asked him an endless array of repetitive questions, run a battery of tests, contacted his own doctor to confer on his condition and concluded exactly what Ian had expected they would. After he'd explained what little he knew of his childhood before his adoptive mother had brought him to America, the hospital's medical team deduced that the incident was a flashback to past trauma. They advised therapy.

He replied that he'd *had* therapy, a lot of it. Glynis McNeill, the only mother he'd ever known, had adopted him at the estimated age of ten from an orphanage in Krasnoyarsk, Russia. She'd named him Ian, after her deceased father, and given him her last name.

More important, Glynis had lavished time and attention on him. Fifty years old and unmarried when she adopted him, his mother got him plastic surgery for the worst of his scars and therapy for his PTSD. Until a few hours ago, his early child-hood had remained mostly a blank. What memo-ries he did have were of the orphanage, a hospital and random, bloody flashes of the bear attack-ing him.

And now, he had the new memory of a brother named Matt, a walk in the snow and a white ro-dent with pale tan stripes leading him off into the woods.

"You're right," he told the doctors. "I survived a bear attack when I was a child. The incident today was a flashback and it's over and I'm fine. I'll be even better once you let me go home."

Dr. Cummings, who seemed to be in charge of his care today, wanted to know if he had a thera-pist he saw regularly.

"Not for several years. I had a therapist starting when I was ten or so until I was in my midteens."

Dr. Cummings frowned. "I strongly advise

that you talk to a therapist now about this. It's possible that the incident today will have an ongoing effect—more suppressed memories could surface, and any number of emotional reactions could occur that you will need help processing. Not to mention headaches and the like. You can contact your regular doctor for a referral, or we can provide you one today."

"I'll handle it." And *not* by seeing a shrink. If more memories surfaced, so be it. As for any processing, he could manage that fine on his own.

"Good enough." Dr. Cummings dipped his head in a nod.

After the tests and consultations, Ian ended up in a curtained-off ER bed. Ella and Abby settled into the chairs on either side of him as they waited for someone to come in and release him.

When he asked for his phone, Ella produced it from the plastic bag of his clothes and belongings. He checked messages, replying to one from his girlfriend, Lucinda.

The minute Lucinda learned he'd spent most of the afternoon in the hospital, she shot him a reply:

Why didn't you SAY something, Ian?

I'm fine, really.

Did it even occur to you that I might want to be there for you?

It's not necessary.

Yes, it is. I'm on my way.

You do not need to come. I mean it, there's no big deal.

But Lucinda wasn't having that. I'm coming over there.

He shook his head at his phone. He'd just about reached that point with her, the one he always got to with the women he dated—the point where he faced the fact that it didn't work and it wouldn't work—and the time had come for Lucinda and him to part ways.

With a weary huff of breath, Ian set the phone on the bed tray. "You two should just go," he advised Ella and Abby. "I'll call the car service when they finally get around to letting me out of here. It will be fine."

Abby stuck out her chin at him. "No way am I leaving you."

Ella shook her head and pinned him with those eyes that were even bigger and darker brown than her daughter's. "I've called Philip." Philip was

Ella's ex-husband, Abby's father. "He'll take Abby and I'll stick around."

"Mom!" Abby made three full syllables out of the word. "I'm not leaving Ian." Her sweet face crumpled. "And I'll never make anyone face their fears again." She would be bursting into tears any minute now if he didn't do something.

He held out a hand. "Come here."

She put her soft fingers in his and grumbled, "What?"

"You did nothing wrong and, as you can see, I'm okay. A hundred tests they did on me. If there was anything that wrong with me, they wouldn't be planning on sending me home."

"Oh, Ian! I was so wrong. I've *traumatized* you."

"No, you haven't."

"I *have*. You've come through so much and I've only made it worse. You could be scarred emotionally—I mean, even more than before—for the rest of your life. I'll never forgive myself…" She threw herself on him.

He gathered her in as Ella looked on patiently. "It's okay, Abby." She smelled of red licorice, dust and something faintly floral, and that made him smile. "There's nothing to blame yourself for. Whatever happened to me when I was younger than you are, I got through it and ended up safe and sound right here in New York. Now I'm living the good life, going to Knicks games with you." He stroked her light brown hair. "It really is okay."

"I just think I need to stay."

Ella spoke up then. "It's no problem. *I'll* stay. You have tap class."

Abby pulled out of his hold and whirled to face her mother. "I can skip. It's only for fun and enrichment, like you always say." Three years ago, Abby had started taking acting and dance classes, planning a Broadway career. Since then, she'd changed her lifetime ambition to becoming a children's book author, but she still enjoyed the dancing. "I just don't feel so fun right now. Enrichment can wait."

"What's this about skipping your dance class?" Philip Haralson, tall and thin with the same light brown hair as his daughter, stood in the gap between the privacy curtains.

Five minutes later, still reluctant and more than a little bit sulky, Abby followed her dad out.

That left just Ian and Ella.

The room fell silent—a relaxed, companionable silence.

Ian knew he should insist that Ella leave, too. But Ell had a way about her, both steady and calm. He liked sitting quietly with her. He also enjoyed talking with her. He liked the way her mind worked, her savvy ideas, her dry sense of humor, her reasonable, no-nonsense approach to life. Ella would call him on his crap, and yet somehow when she did, it never felt like she judged him—more like she held him to account, kept him honest.

Looking at her gave him pleasure, too. He liked her wavy, seal-brown hair and those steady dark eyes. It felt good to have her there.

Bald truth: he didn't want her to go.

Another half hour went by. They laughed together about how the doctor would probably never come. Ian would be stuck here in an ER cubicle at Manhattan General for the rest of his life.

He'd just decided to confide in her, to share the new memory that had come to him right after the grueling flashback at the zoo, when he glanced over and saw Lucinda standing in the gap between the curtains. She had a dangerous expression on her gorgeous face—like someone had just insulted her and she couldn't wait to start ranting in retaliation.

Ian tried to head her off. "Sweetheart, come on over here and—"

"Don't you 'sweetheart' me." She sent a withering glare at Ella and then swung her gaze back on him. "You called *her* and then took *hours* to even answer my text?"

He started to tell her to knock off the attitude.

But Ella spoke first. "He didn't call me," she said, her voice kind and reasonable, which was way more than Lucinda deserved. "He was with Abby, at the park. When he passed out, *Abby* called me."

Lucinda swung her glittering green eyes his way again. "It's worse than a stepchild," she muttered, "you and that kid. It's over, Ian. I'm out of here." With a shake of her tumbling blond curls, she spun on her red-soled, sky-high heel and vanished from sight.

Ella drew a slow breath. "I'll talk to her."

"Let her go," he commanded.

Ella pointed at him. "Stay. There." She raced after Lucinda.

Ella caught up with Ian's girlfriend at the elevator. "Come on, Lucinda." She pitched her voice low, making it just between the two of them. No, she didn't especially care for Lucinda, who wore her drama-queen ways as a badge of honor, but she also didn't want to be the reason for Ian's breakup with the woman.

"Please, Lucinda. Don't go running off angry…"

The woman whirled on her. Getting right up in Ella's face, she whisper-shouted, "Forget it. I've had enough. I'm done with Ian. As for you, everyone knows you're in love with him. It's pathetic. You need to get a life."

The elevator doors parted. Lucinda got on the empty car. Ella stood there with her mouth hanging open as the doors slid shut on Ian's angry girlfriend—correction. *Ex*-girlfriend, apparently.

When Ella got back to Ian's cubicle, she found him standing in the split between the curtains waiting for her, his big arms crossed over his broad chest, his muscular, hairy legs sticking out below his hospital gown, wearing those silly nonskid socks the hospital had given him. Was he naked under that gown? Probably. It tied down the back. He must have hesitated to set off after her and give the nurses a view of his bare ass.

When she reached him, he demanded, "What did she say?"

Ella ordered her heart rate to slow and her palms to stop sweating. "Nothing important—oh, she might have mentioned again that she's through with you."

He dared to smirk. "What do you know? Something Lucinda and I can agree on."

Ella drew a slower breath. At least he hadn't demanded that she tell him everything the woman had said.

And as for the demise of his relationship with Lucinda, *quelle surprise*. Ian had never been the kind of guy who got married and settled down. He dated exclusively, but none of them lasted. With Ian, it was a revolving door of beautiful women.

Lucinda, apparently, had reached her expiration date on the Ian McNeill relationship wheel.

Ella tried. She tried so hard.

But that night, the next day and the day after that, she couldn't make herself stop obsessing over what Lucinda had said.

It's not true, no way, she kept reassuring herself. *It can't be true. It's ridiculous. Me and Ian? Uh-uh. Impossible...*

By Friday, four days after the incident, she still hadn't stopped fixating on Lucinda's whispered taunt. That day, she left the office at a little before noon to meet her longtime friend Marisol Hardy, whose daughter, Charlotte, was Abby's bestie. Ella and Marisol had met in childbirth class, and now their daughters took hip-hop and tap together. Marisol knew Ian casually. She'd dropped in at the office more than once over the years, and Ian always showed up at the girls' dance recitals.

Bottom line, Marisol would put Ella's mind at ease. They would laugh together over the mere idea that Ella might have a thing for her boss and longtime friend—let alone have fallen in love with the man.

That Friday, they met for lunch at Telegraphe Café, midway between their two apartments in Chelsea. Once they were settled at a small table with tall iced teas and caprese salads, Ella told Marisol what had happened at the hospital that Monday, concluding with Lucinda's preposterous parting shot.

"I mean, where in the world could she have come up with that one?" Ella demanded. "Ian's my friend and I love him dearly, but you know how he is, ten dates maximum—more likely five or six—and the woman is outta there. I want real, lasting love, and Ian is not the kind of guy to pin any hopes on. A woman who falls for him is just begging for heartbreak."

Ella paused to nibble a bite of bread, tossing the crust down in disgust. "Let alone, he's my boss. *And* two years younger than me. How many ways is he all wrong for me?" She picked up her fork, speared a bite of her salad and stuck it in her mouth. Once she'd finished chewing and swallowing, she concluded with, "No. Just no." And then indulged in a sip of iced tea while she waited for her friend to start laughing.

But Marisol didn't laugh. In fact, she winced.

Ella put her glass down and demanded, "What was that? Did you just *wince* at me?" Marisol, clearly uncomfortable, guided a corkscrew of rust-brown hair behind her ear and sagged against the banquette cushion. "You did, then?" Ella's voice sounded plaintive to her own ears. "You *winced* at me."

"What do you want me to tell you?"

Ella knew then that she should just leave it alone. But somehow, she couldn't. "I want the truth, of course."

Marisol gave her the side-eye and then let out a tired little sigh. "You *are* in love with Ian," she said softly. "You have been for years."

Like an acid bath, her friend's words washed over her, burning. She ate another bite of salad and followed that up with a second sip of tea. "Why did you have to tell me that?"

"Um, you asked?"

With her fork, Ella nudged a bit of mozzarella off a tomato slice. "Point taken—and you know what? Let's not talk about it anymore."

"Ella…"

"No, really. I mean it. We need to leave the subject of Ian McNeill far behind."

Marisol reached across the table, caught the back of Ella's hand briefly and gave it a squeeze. "Okay."

Ella's friend was as good as her word. They left it at that.

But Ella didn't really leave it. For the rest of the

day, she thought about Ian constantly, swinging from absolute denial to a sense of growing horror that she might have somehow, impossibly, fallen in love with her commitment-averse friend and boss.

At least Ian was out of the office that afternoon. She didn't have to see him or speak with him.

Still, her misery and confusion only got worse.

After school that day, Abby went to her dad's for the weekend. She forgot her retainer and sent Ella a text as she was leaving the office asking if maybe, *please* she might run the device over to Philip's.

It wasn't a big deal. Philip and his family lived just around the corner from Ella. As soon as she got home, Ella grabbed the retainer case from the night table by Abby's bed and went on over there.

Philip answered the door. "Ella." He gave her a warm smile of welcome. "Come on in."

"Thanks, I have to run." She held out the retainer case. "Just here to drop off the usual."

Philip studied her face and frowned. "What's the matter?"

"Nothing."

He stepped out into the hallway with her and pulled the door shut behind him, raising his index and middle finger and aiming them both at the space just over her nose. "You've got the lines between your eyes." He'd always claimed she scrunched her eyebrows together when something was bothering her.

Yeah, her ex knew far too much about her. The same age and the same grade through school, they'd been best friends since they were nine, when Ella's parents had died in a boating accident and her aunt Clara in New York City had taken her in. The Haralson family had lived in the same building as her aunt.

No, she'd never fallen in love with Philip, nor he with her. It was friendship between them, pure and strong and simple, always had been. They'd had a lot in common, Ella and Philip. Both shy and semi-invisible at school, they'd sworn to be besties forever.

And at the age of eighteen, they'd hatched a scheme to experiment with sex together—in order that when they finally did fall in love, they would know what they were doing in bed.

A slipup on the contraception front had resulted in Abby. Under pressure from Philip's parents, whom Ella had always adored, they'd caved. She and Philip got married right after graduation from high school, while secretly vowing to each other that they would divorce as soon as they both finished college. And they'd kept that vow, too, splitting up as planned, much to the disappointment of the elder Haralsons.

Philip had found his true love, Chloe, a year later. Now, he and Chloe had two adorable little girls, Zoe and Leah. Some people had all the luck.

Philip narrowed his eyes at her. It was his *I can see inside your head* look. "Talk to me."

"Philip, I'm fine."

"Something's bothering you."

"I have to get going…"

"Wait." He blinked and loomed closer. "Now I get it. You've met someone."

"Stop." He really was a sweetheart, and he wanted her to find her true love as much as she did. But she refused to get into this with him. In fact, she felt minimally grateful Philip had no clue that her "someone" might be Ian, of all people. "There's no one, I promise you," she insisted, trying hard to believe it. And then she went up on tiptoe and brushed a kiss on his cheek. "Gotta go. Hugs to Chloe and the girls. Tell our daughter I love her, and I'll see her Monday after work."

She turned and got out of there before he could say another word.

Down the street, she got takeout from her favorite falafel place and carried the food back to her too-quiet apartment, where her mind would not stop arguing with itself over the scary possibility that the man she wanted might actually be Ian.

Oh, dear God. What if it *was* Ian? What if she did love him?

What if Ian was her "one"?

That man would never commit. In the past, she'd always found it thoroughly annoying when Philip quizzed her on her love life—or lack thereof.

Now, though? Downright depressing.

Oh, God. Please, no.

She couldn't be in love with Ian. She *wouldn't* be in love with Ian.

Denial. Definitely. Denial was the only way to go.

Monday, at the office, she managed pretty well. She dealt with Ian the same way she always did, with the usual wry humor, honesty and friendly respect. They were a great team. He ran the business, and she backed him up and communicated his decisions to their employees. In meetings, she spoke up when she felt that he or their CFO, David Karnavan, were on the wrong track. Both men took her seriously.

That day, she behaved as though nothing had changed. It worked. No one seemed to suspect she might be freaking out internally. Most important, she felt certain that Ian didn't have a clue as to the chaos in her head and her heart.

However…

It did seem to her that, since that awful day

when he'd ended up in the ER and she'd found out what she never wanted to know from his now ex-girlfriend…

Well, looking back, it seemed to Ella that from that day on, something strange was going on with Ian, too.

He seemed preoccupied, like something bothered him, nagged at him. Whatever troubled him, he hid it well in meetings. But sometimes she would see him in his corner office alone, staring off into the middle distance.

After a couple more days of that strangeness, she asked him outright if anything was wrong.

He put on a puzzled expression. "No idea what you're talking about, Ell. I'm good. Nothing out of the ordinary going on."

She would have pressed him a little, but he started in about her upcoming trip to the factory in Minneapolis. Six years ago, when Glynis was still at the helm, they'd moved production to the Twin Cities to keep costs down. Now Ella flew out there at least twice a month to check in with the design, development and manufacturing teams.

By the time they'd talked through Ian's questions for the design team, the workday had ended. She went home more certain than ever that something weighed on his mind.

Eventually, he *would* tell her. Her supposed

hopeless love for him aside, she knew him. Though he rarely trusted anyone, he did trust her. He would bust himself to her eventually.

Thursday, she flew to Minneapolis, returning after seven on Friday night. From the airport, she went straight home.

Early Saturday, she picked up Abby at Philip's. They shopped for groceries, after which they cleaned the apartment they both loved. It had gorgeous old pine floors, an original fireplace and a view of the Empire State Building—if you stood in the living area window just so. The thousand-square-foot two-bedroom co-op had cost Ella a lot. And it was worth every penny, too.

Around five, Abby went back to Philip's for pizza and a family movie night.

At a little after six, Ella settled on the sofa with the remote. She was scrolling the Netflix options when someone buzzed from downstairs. She got up and answered.

It was Ian. "You busy?"

Chapter Three

Despite her annoying hyperawareness of him lately, Ella smiled to herself. *About time*, she thought. Whatever he had on his mind, she would do her best to help him get to the bottom of it.

She buzzed him up and then waited in her open doorway for him to appear.

He came around the corner from the elevator. The sight of him made her heart ache—and not because of her own confusion over her feelings for him.

No. She ached for his sake alone. His thick, dark blond hair, cut long on top and close at the sides, looked kind of scrambled. He must have been shoving his fingers in it. His blue eyes had shadows under them, and his beard scruff seemed a little longer than usual.

Her friend was a mess, and she wanted to help.

Marching right up to her, he muttered, "Don't look at me like that."

"Like what?"

He scowled. "Where's Abby?"

"At her dad's."

"Good. She doesn't need to hear this crap."

What crap? she almost demanded. But no. Better to let him open up about the problem in his own good time.

They regarded each other. After several seconds, he demanded, "You gonna let me in?"

She moved aside and gestured him forward with a wave of her hand. "Coffee?"

"Got anything stronger?"

She followed him down the narrow entry hallway to the living area, where he dropped to the sofa with an audible sigh, as though he carried the weight of the world on those broad shoulders.

She offered, "Vodka? White wine?"

"The vodka. Just ice."

"Lime?"

"Perfect."

She poured one for herself, too, and joined him on the sofa.

He took the drink and sipped. "It's good."

"You're welcome. So, what's going on?"

He leaned forward, braced his elbows on his spread knees, the glass dangling between them in both hands, and stared down into the clear liquid as though the answers to deep questions lurked between the chunks of crushed ice. "I need to talk."

"Yeah, I figured."

He slanted her a wry glance. "Sorry about the other day. I was still hoping... I don't know. That if I stayed in denial long enough, the whole thing would just go away."

She had to hold back a laugh. After all, she felt the same—about the grim possibility that she loved him in a way destined to end badly for her. She prompted, "But it *didn't* go away..."

He nodded, head down again, eyes focused on the glass between his hands. "I mean, you asked me, the other day. And I lied and said there was nothing. But then I kept thinking that I really do need to talk to someone, and I don't even want to get going with a therapist again." He turned those blue eyes directly on her. "I just need to talk it out with a friend."

She resisted the urge to put her hand on his knee. After what Lucinda had said, well, it just felt wrong to touch him, like she'd be indulging her secret, unacceptable desires.

God. This was awful. It shouldn't be happening, these feelings she suddenly realized she had for this man. He had his problems—with getting close, with commitment. And yet he'd always been good to her, *there* for her. He treated her daughter like a princess. They all—at work, Philip and Chloe, everyone in their circle of colleagues, family and friends—jokingly called Ian "Abby's second dad."

But it wasn't a joke, not really. Whatever happened, Ian would make sure that Abby had whatever she needed to get a great start in life.

"Just tell me," Ella said softly. "Just get it out."

He shook his head. "You should probably suggest that I pull it together and then send me home."

Enough. She was so done with waiting for him to open up. Time to give him a push in the right direction. "Stop it. You're here. You didn't come just so I could tell you to get over it and go away. I mean it, Ian. Talk."

He took another sip of his drink, a big one, no doubt to brace himself, and then he said, "Since that day at the zoo, I've been remembering."

At his gruffly spoken words, the breath seemed to flee her body. All these years he'd lived in the dark when it came to his early childhood. She dragged in a giant gulp of air. "About your life before the bear attack?"

"Yeah."

"Tell me. Everything."

He started talking about Russia, the stuff she already knew from bits of information he and Glynis had shared with her over the years. He spoke of the hospital where he woke in pain, covered in bandages, not knowing his own name, with everyone speaking a language he didn't understand.

"And the orphanage…" His voice trailed off. "I've always remembered way too much about my life there, too…"

He'd told her a few years ago that the other children were hardened, either completely withdrawn or dangerous, that the women who cared for them had grim faces, with too many kids to look after and no time to give comfort or hugs. He'd learned quickly that drawing the attention of those women would only earn him a slap and a harsh reprimand—or worse.

On the sofa, Ian had fallen silent. Again, Ella found herself holding her breath. He remained quiet. She drew in air and let it out slowly and recalled the old story, of how, at the orphanage, they'd given him the name Nicolas Ivanov, but he'd refused to answer to it—refused to speak at all. Even later, after he'd picked up enough Russian to communicate if he'd wanted to, he'd felt safer just letting them all believe he was mute.

Ian told more of the story Ella already knew. "Then Glynis showed up to find a child to adopt."

Glynis had looked at the boy they called Nicolas, and he'd gazed back at her and he'd *known* that she was good, that she was kind. And then he'd heard her speak and he knew he had to find a way to go home with her, that he was an American—though from what part of the country or who his people were, he had no clue. He'd felt bleakly certain that she wouldn't take him, that she would want a baby, as everyone did, a pretty, pure, happy little baby.

"No would want some scarred-up kid who never said a word to anyone." He knocked back another big gulp of his drink. "But she looked at me and I stared at her and I saw in her eyes then that she felt what I felt." Both he and Glynis had described their first eye contact as a connection, an understanding. "And I knew with zero doubt that she would do it, take *me* with her instead of the baby she'd come for…" He seemed to run out of words.

"She was one of a kind, your mother." Glynis, who'd been raised in the foster care system after her only parent, her father, had died, never let her tough start in life get her down. Always upbeat and ready to take on the world, Glynis had fallen from a ladder trying to change a lightbulb in her Upper East Side brownstone. She'd hit her head and died instantly. That was a little over a year ago now.

She'd left her adopted son everything she owned, including the toy business she'd loved.

Ian nodded, eyes vacant, gaze fixed on the hallway. "I miss her."

"Me, too." Ella waited. He continued to stare blankly down the hallway for several long seconds. Carefully, she prompted, "But about your life before that, here in the States?"

"Yeah. About who I was before…" His burnished eyebrows scrunched together. He downed the rest of his drink and held out the glass. "Just one more?"

She traded him for hers, which she'd yet to taste.

"Thanks." He held the fresh drink between his big, long-fingered hands, as if just the feel of the cold glass steadied him. "Okay, so within a few days of losing it at the zoo, I'd remembered a bunch of random stuff about my family here in the US, that their last name was Bravo, that we lived in some little town on the Oregon coast called Valentine Bay."

Sudden tears blurred her vision—for him, for the childhood he'd lost. For the family he would finally have a chance to reconnect with, at last, after all this time. "Ian. That's amazing. That's so big."

"Big." He scoffed. "Too bad I'm not coping very well."

"Of course you are. I mean, you're dealing

with it. Don't be hard on yourself. Give yourself a break. You're talking about it, you're facing it. And you have to do that in your own time and your own way."

He turned his gaze to her then. A ghost of a smile haunted his gorgeous mouth, with its full bottom lip and distinct cupid's bow. "You're a good friend, Ell. Steady. Solid."

Steady and solid. He meant it as compliment, though she couldn't help hearing it as something else altogether. *Steady and solid*, huh? He might as well just call her dull and dependable.

"Yeah, I'm a rock, all right."

"True that." He sent her a wry smile.

She reminded herself that she needed to keep her own inner turmoil out of this. Right now, her focus belonged on what he needed as her friend.

Ian set his half-finished second drink on the coffee table and folded his hands between his spread knees. "So anyway, I spent a whole night, dusk till dawn last week, scouring the internet for whatever I could find about the Bravo family of Valentine Bay. And then I took what I'd remembered and what I'd learned online to a private investigator. Yesterday, the PI sent me a big file packed with more than I could ever want to know about my lost family and the boy I used to be."

Rising, he went to the window next to the sofa.

He knew where to stand for the view of the Art Deco skyscraper with the giant antenna on top. As he stared at the marvel of twentieth-century architecture, he rattled off facts.

"My name was Finnegan Bravo—called Finn. I was sixth-born of nine children—five boys, four girls. My parents apparently had a thing for world travel and died in a tsunami on a trip to Thailand two years after I disappeared. I vanished in Siberia near the city of Irkutsk when I was eight." His gaze shifted to her briefly.

And then he stared out the window some more. "Irkutsk, by the way, is almost seven hundred miles from Krasnoyarsk, where I woke up in the hospital God only knows how long after I wandered away from my family. And how I traveled all that distance? I don't have a clue. There was an extensive search for the lost Finn Bravo, though, and a large reward offered to anyone who found me. My ending up so far from where I was last seen explains why nobody ever turned me in to collect the money."

She reminded him, "Plus, you never spoke until after Glynis brought you to New York. The Russians really had no way of knowing who you were or where you'd come from."

"Right. I had no idea who I was, either. And I trusted no one." Shoving his hands in the pockets of his dark-wash Italian-made jeans, he turned from the window to meet her eyes, that beautiful, rueful smile flickering across his face again. "I stole your drink, didn't I? Sorry."

"No problem. I know where to get more." She picked up the glass from the coffee table and held it out to him.

He took it, had another sip. "I can't stop thinking about flying out there to Oregon, about meeting them—at the same time, though, I just can't see myself doing that."

Ella couldn't let that go. "You need to do it."

"Ell." He said her name—the nickname only he ever called her—so tenderly. *Friendship*, she reminded herself sternly. *That's what we have. That's who we are together.* He chided, "You don't get to decide if I meet them or not."

"I know, but Ian. Consider the possibilities. You have brothers and sisters. You have *family*. A big family." What she wouldn't give for a big family. When her mom and dad died, there had only been her dad's much-older sister, Aunt Clara, between Ella and the foster care system. A good person who did her duty by Ella and stepped up as Ella's guardian, Aunt Clara had avoided strong emotions and steered clear of physical contact. With Aunt Clara, hugs were rare. That first year with her aunt, Ella had cried in her room alone a lot. She would have given just about anything to have had a brother or sister to hold on to.

"I don't know them," Ian insisted. "Glynis was my mom. She was enough."

Ella wanted to shake him. "Ian, love...*expands*. You won't love Glynis less if you meet your birth family—and okay, maybe you won't even like them when you meet them. But maybe you will. And they'll *know* things about the boy you were once. They're your history, just waiting out there in Oregon for you to discover them."

Was she pushing too hard? Definitely. She really did want him to do this his own way. But when she thought about him *not* meeting his lost family, well, that just felt so wrong. He *had* to go.

She pushed some more. "You need to meet them, to get to know them..."

He gazed down at her indulgently, the way he looked at Abby sometimes, like she was just so cute, so amusing in her youth and innocence. "May I remind you that I passed out just from watching a couple of frolicking grizzly bears from thirty feet away through a shatterproof protective viewing screen?"

"You're not going pass out when you meet your brothers and sisters."

"You can't be sure of that."

For a moment, they just looked at each other. It was, essentially, a face-off. A stare-down.

He broke the silence. "Hard fact. I'm not doing that alone."

She got it then. "You want me to go with you. That's why you're here. To get me to go with you." She laughed, but her throat felt tight with feelings she refused to examine too closely.

He handed her drink back. "Will you? Ell, I need a friend for this."

"Of course you do." Lucinda's cruel taunt echoed through her mind… *Everyone knows you're in love with him. It's pathetic.*

He'd said it himself. He needed a *friend*. And she hardly understood her own heart at this point. Flying off to the West Coast with him? Probably not the best choice for her emotional well-being right now.

But it wasn't about her. It was about Ian and what she would give to see that he got what he needed.

A lot. She would give a lot.

She brought the glass to her lips and drank the rest. "Of course I'll go."

"Thank you." Ian felt grateful for a friend like Ella, who didn't so much as hesitate when he'd asked her to help him meet the family he wasn't even sure he wanted to know.

"When do we leave?" she asked brightly, so obviously eager and ready to reunite him with a bunch of people he felt nothing for.

"Soon. I'm thinking Thursday, returning the following Monday. I want to get in and get out." The whole thing made him edgy—unnerved. He agreed with Ella that he needed to do it, but that didn't mean he had to like it.

"Abby will want to go," she said, after which they shook their heads simultaneously and said "No" at the same time.

Ella added, "You're right that we have no idea how things will shake out when we get there. *I* think it will be great, and if it is, maybe one of these days you'll want to fly her out there with you."

"Maybe." He could not see that ever happening but saw no need to make a point of it. Right now, he just wanted to get the whole thing over with.

She grinned at him. "You look so uncomfortable."

"Yeah, well. It's not what I would call a pleasure trip."

"True." Ella shrugged. "So then, as for Abby, I'll tell her what's going on, that you've remembered enough about your birth family to pay them a visit. Is that okay?"

"That'll work."

"She can stay with her dad and she has school anyway, so we don't have to get too specific with her about why she can't come with."

"Good plan."

Ella wiggled her empty glass. "Another drink?"

"Better not."

She set the glass next to his on the coffee table. "Ian, it's going to work out. You'll be glad you went." Her dark eyes gleamed, and her pretty, soft mouth had curved in a happy smile. She seemed excited about the whole thing. He wished he could share her enthusiasm for meeting a bunch of strangers in the interest of reforging family bonds.

"I hope so." He tried not to sound as full of doubt and discomfort as he felt.

Abby called him Sunday morning. "Ian! You've been remembering…" She sounded thrilled at the very idea. "I should come over. I know you need to talk about it."

No, he didn't. "Can't, sorry. Got a busy Sunday lined up." It was true, more or less. He planned to spend several hours at the office that day, getting ahead of the workload in preparation for taking three weekdays off.

"Mom says I can't go to Oregon with you." Abby used her pouty voice.

"School is important."

"Yeah, right—and I guess this means making you face your fears wasn't *all* bad, after all?" Now she sounded equal parts hesitant and hopeful.

He wondered if anything good could possibly come from meeting relatives he hadn't seen since he was someone else entirely. But Abby needed reassurance about the incident at the zoo. He put on his best imitation of a happy voice and gave it to her. "You're right. It was a good thing. Thanks for, uh, giving me a nudge in the right direction."

"I still feel bad about it."

"Don't."

"That day, when your eyes rolled back, and you crumpled to the ground? I couldn't stop screaming. I thought, maybe, you were never going to wake up."

"Well, I did wake up, and I'm good as new." And Abby Haralson would never feel guilty or unhappy—not if he could do anything about it. "Stop blaming yourself. It all turned out fine."

She blew out a heavy breath. "I guess you really are okay."

"I am, I promise you."

"And you'll get to meet your family finally, after all this time."

"Yay."

She laughed. "Oh, Ian. Sometimes you're such a Grumpy Gus."

He made a grumpy sound, just to prove her right.

She started in about the book she was reading and then moved on to a story she'd begun writing in which a girl very much like her discovered she could time travel and saved the world by changing history. He praised her storytelling skills and admired her vivid imagination.

When they said goodbye twenty minutes later, she sounded happy and upbeat. He might only be her second dad, but he congratulated himself on doing a decent job of lifting her spirits and banishing the last of her guilt over what had happened at the zoo.

First thing Monday, he had Audrey, his assistant, book him and Ella flights to and from Portland, Oregon. A rental car would be waiting at PDX and Ian would drive them the rest of the way to the little town on the Pacific up near the border with Washington State. Audrey had them staying at a hotel right there in town.

How bad could it be? he kept asking himself bleakly. Five days out of his life to meet a bunch of people he'd had no memory of until a couple of weeks ago—five days, two of which would be for travel.

He could do this. And then he could say he'd met his birth family.

Ella strolled into his office at nine thirty Monday morning, dropped into the chair opposite his desk and sipped from the Black Fox Coffee Company to-go cup she'd carried in with her. "So. Did that investigator you hired give you phone numbers?" He must have looked confused, because she clarified, "Phone numbers for any of your brothers and sisters?"

He guessed where she was leading him, and he didn't plan to go there. But still, he answered honestly, "Yeah."

She took a slow sip of coffee. "Then you'll call them, let them know you're coming?"

"I'll call them when we get there."

Ella became very still. He tried not to smile. He knew that look on her face. She thought he should contact them beforehand but also knew that once he'd made up his mind about something, he rarely changed course.

"Ian." She spoke in a solemn yet coaxing voice. "It seems only fair to give them a heads-up. Look at it from their point of view. It's going to be a shock, to say the least. A little warning wouldn't hurt."

She was right—as usual.

Didn't matter. He would face the Bravos in Oregon and not until then. "Ell. I don't want to call ahead."

"Why not?"

"I see no need to drag it out."

"What if you can't reach any of them when we get there?"

"I have eight siblings—all but two of them married, all of them living either in that little town or close by. Odds are someone will be available when I decide to get in touch."

"But—" He cut her off with a shake of his head and, finally, she accepted his decision. "Well, then. Guess you're not calling ahead." She rose and turned for the door.

"See you at ten," he said gently to her retreating back.

"I know when the morning meeting is, Ian," she replied downright snippily without pausing or glancing back.

Snippy was good. Snippy meant she wouldn't be getting on him again about calling ahead, and that worked for him.

More than once that week, Ella considered backing out of the Portland trip. Being Ian's best buddy and emotional support for five days seemed like such a bad idea for her right now.

She had her own issues lately—issues that mostly consisted of the need to constantly deny the remote possibility that his most recent ex-girlfriend had been right, that Ella had made the giant mistake of falling for the ultimate unavailable man. All that denial took a whole bunch of effort already, when she only had to deal with him at work. She didn't need five days of constant proximity to the guy messing with her focus on pretending that bitch Lucinda didn't know her ass from up.

But every time she convinced herself that she needed to march into Ian's office and let him know she'd changed her mind about going with him, well, she just couldn't do it.

He could be a jerk. But he was *her* jerk—in a friends-only way. It mattered, that a woman stuck by a friend.

Thus, on Thursday at nine in the morning, they boarded their flight to Oregon. The first-class seats were roomy and comfortable, the brunch delicious. Ian seemed preoccupied and reluctant to chat.

Fine with her. She put on her sleep mask and adjusted her seat.

When she woke, Ian had his black-rimmed glasses on and his laptop opened—working, as usual.

He glanced over at her and gave her his beautiful smile—the real one that he saved for the small group of people who had his trust. She didn't get that smile often. Nobody did—except Abby, of course.

Ella basked in that smile, though the voice in her head that lately sounded like Lucinda taunted, *Give it up, fool. He doesn't do lasting relationships and a fling with him is a bad, bad idea.*

Not that Ian would want a fling with Ella, anyway. He considered her a good friend and colleague. She was no Lucinda. She lacked the bombshell packaging *and* the disposability. No way he would sacrifice her true value to him for something as easy to get as sex.

"Sleep well?" he asked.

"I did, thanks." Had she drooled on herself? She made a quick inventory. No spots on her shirt, nothing on her face. Wrinkling her nose at him, she asked, "Did I snore?"

"Not a peep." He leaned a little closer. She got a whiff of that expensive cologne he wore that smelled of grass and deep woods, all cool and somehow soothing. "Want some champagne?"

She shook her head. "Too dehydrating on a flight. But maybe with dinner."

"You're so well behaved." He still leaned into her, his elbow on the wide, padded armrest between their seats. She could see the silvery rays fanning out from his pupils through the blue irises. And she felt better about everything. What did Lucinda know, anyway—or Marisol, for that matter?

Ella loved Ian, yeah. As a dear friend. Nothing else going on here. Tagging along for moral support as he reunited with his birth family would be good for him and a nice change of pace for her.

"On second thought," she said, "bring on the bubbly."

Did she get a little tipsy before they touched down in Portland? Maybe.

Ian enjoyed a single scotch rocks while she sipped her champagne, and they whispered together about Abby's next dance recital and the new stuffed toy, Woodrow the warthog, that Patch&Pebble would be launching in time for the holiday market.

They landed in Portland right on time. Forty-five minutes later, they headed for Valentine Bay in the Lexus SUV Audrey had rented for them.

The drive took an hour and a half. At a little before five, they checked into the Isabel Inn, a gorgeous, shingled New England–style hotel a short walk from the ocean in Valentine Bay. Audrey had booked them a two-bedroom suite, with a large, beautifully furnished deck that faced the

Pacific and offered access directly to the beach. The hotel also boasted a dining room where the chef prepared well-reviewed seasonal fare. They had dinner reservations for six thirty.

Before retreating to her own room to settle in, Ella tried again to convince Ian he ought to give one of the Bravos a call.

"It's a big deal, Ian, your showing up here in Oregon. Your family deserves a heads-up."

He stood at the end of the sand-colored sofa, next to the coffee table stacked with large, beautifully illustrated books about the Oregon coast and graced with a white orchid soaring out of a tea-green pot on a slender, curving stem. He had the remote in hand, his eyes on the flat screen over the fireplace as he flipped through channels. "Tomorrow."

"Ian, I just think—"

"Stop." He sent her that look, the one that said no way would she get him to do that and she'd better give it up now.

"All righty, then." She flicked him a wave over her shoulder and marched through the door to her room, pulling it closed behind her—quietly, too, though the urge to give it a nice, hard slam vibrated through her, making her clench her teeth and growl low in her throat.

* * *

Ian turned off the flat screen and tossed the remote on the sofa.

Maybe Ella had a point. He probably should call. The PI he'd hired had reported that, over the years, the Bravos had put feelers out everywhere for him. They'd tried to find him.

And they never would have. Not without him remembering them first. Whatever series of circumstances had carried him from that snowy path near Irkutsk to a hospital hundreds of miles away had severed the connection between Finn Bravo and the boy who became Nicolas Ivanov and, finally, Ian McNeill. His refusal to speak for all that time hadn't helped, either.

The Bravos must think him dead by now. Showing up on their doorstep out of the blue might cause someone to suffer a heart attack.

A call first would help ease the way.

Ian slid his phone from his pocket and brought up his contacts list. He'd entered all the Bravo family phone numbers the PI had sent him. Daniel was the eldest brother, so he would probably be the top choice to try first. Ian stared at the screen, his thumb hovering over the phone icon next to Daniel Bravo's name.

"No." He dropped the phone on a book of landscape photographs, grabbed his laptop and went to his room, where he tossed the computer on the bed, kicked off his shoes, threw his jacket on a chair and flopped down on the mattress.

After ten minutes of staring at the ceiling, wondering why he'd let himself become a total wreck over this situation, he sat up, grabbed the laptop and emailed some questions to David, his CFO. After reading through David's response, he shut the device and flopped to his back again.

The ceiling hadn't changed one bit since the last time he stared at it.

Eventually, he got up and padded back into the living area. Scooping up his phone, he keyed in his PIN and stared at Daniel Bravo's name some more.

It had started to rain.

Dropping the phone, he went to the glass door that looked out on the deck, with the beach and the ocean beyond. For a while he stared at the misty sky, at the gulls dipping and soaring over the water, the waves rolling in, leading edges laced with foam.

No, he wasn't calling Daniel Bravo. Tomorrow, he would show up. If some brother or sister fell over dead from the shock, well, then he would have that on his conscience. They would all get through it, somehow.

He just needed to stop thinking about it, stop second-guessing his choices. And Ella needed to stop pressuring him to do what he didn't intend to do.

Out there beyond the deck, on the beach midway to the water's edge, a man and a woman strolled along, holding hands. The breeze blew their hair back, away from their faces. As he watched, the woman laughed, tossing her head, exposing the sleek column of her long neck.

She reminded him of Ella, somehow—the wavy dark hair falling below her shoulders, the slim, leggy body. Had he been too hard on Ella about the phone call?

Probably—okay, yeah. He had.

She'd come all this way to help him get through this grueling meeting-the-lost-family thing. He shouldn't treat her cruelly because she encouraged him to show consideration for the siblings he hadn't seen for twenty years.

And no. That didn't mean he would call ahead and give his lost family fair warning. He wouldn't. He just couldn't deal with any of that right now. Tonight, he needed to relax and get his bearings, get his head in the right space for whatever would go down tomorrow.

But he *would* apologize to Ella for being a jackass.

Before he could think of all the reasons he ought to just leave the poor woman alone until it was time to head over to the dining room for dinner, he spun away from the view of the beach, marched to her door and turned the knob. She hadn't locked it, so he pushed it open.

And found her standing by the bed in a black satin thong and bra to match.

Chapter Four

"Ian!" Ella said his name on a gasp, her coffee-colored eyes wide and startled.

He blinked. "Uh. Sorry. It was open."

With a scowl that hinted she just might punch him in the face, she marched toward him.

Really, his good friend was hot—all lean and smooth and tight, with small, high breasts. Willowy. Yeah. That was the word. She had legs that didn't quit and long, graceful arms.

She walked right up to him. "Did you want something, Ian?"

Did he want something? Right at this moment, he could get ideas. "Er, just wanted you to know.

I get it. I was a douche to you about the whole calling-ahead thing and I'm sorry for that."

"You're sorry." She spoke with zero inflection.

It took a whole lot of effort, but he resisted the temptation to let his gaze meander down her sleek, pretty body and slowly back up again. "I am sorry. Very."

"So then, you *will* call one of your brothers now?"

It took him a second or two to respond to her question. She must have showered. She smelled so good—sweet and a little bit spicy. The urge to sneak a quick glance at all that smoothness lower down kept distracting him. But somehow, he kept his focus locked on her face. "No. Not calling tonight."

"If not tonight, when?"

"I never said I would call ahead."

"Ah. So nothing has changed, then?"

"No. It's only, I'm sorry for being an ass to you about it. That's all."

"Step back, Ian."

"Huh?"

She waited. It took about three seconds for his brain to catch up with his ears. When that happened, he stepped back into the living area of the suite.

"One more thing," she said.

"Of course."

"I know Glynis taught you not to barge into other people's rooms without knocking."

"She did, yes." He felt really guilty, like a kid caught with a mouthful of cookies and crumbs on his shirt. "I'm sorry about that, too—about barging in on you like this. I should have knocked."

"Yes, you should. Do so in the future."

"Definitely. I will."

She gave the door a push, and it closed in his face.

He stood there, staring at the shut door for several long seconds, feeling so strange—aroused, addle-headed and embarrassed, too.

Finally, with a slow, deep breath, he squared his shoulders and turned for his bedroom suite, where he showered and changed into casual gray pants and a white button-up, rolling the sleeves to the elbows and skipping a jacket. The Oregon coast hardly seemed a place where a guy needed a jacket to get seated for dinner.

As he put on his socks and shoes, he tried to clear his mind of troubling thoughts, yet he felt a hum of anticipation. Images of Ella in her little black thong kept popping into his brain. That buzz of heat under his skin wouldn't quite go away.

Not only did he seem to have a sudden case of unforeseen lust for his dear friend and COO, but he hardly knew what to expect when she emerged to go to dinner.

She might still be pissed at him—justifiably so.

But he needn't have worried. At six fifteen, she breezed into the shared room of the suite looking great, wearing a short black dress scattered with white flowers and black ankle boots, the dark silk of her hair falling in soft waves over her shoulders.

She seemed completely relaxed and not the least annoyed with him. And hadn't he always loved that about her? Ella made her point and moved on. She never let weird feelings linger.

As soon as Ian gave her a smile, Ella felt better about everything.

Apparently, he'd gotten past her reaction to him bursting in on her earlier. She'd worried a little that he might hold a grudge for the way she'd scolded him. Really, she shouldn't have been so hard on him. It was painfully clear to her that the prospect of meeting his family again after all this time had stressed him out in a big way.

She needed to keep firmly in mind that she'd come on this trip to support Ian, to help him keep some semblance of emotional equilibrium. He'd never excelled at dealing with his feelings. This situation had to be hell for him.

Yeah, it had shocked her to glance over and see

him framed in the open doorway, gaping at her in her underwear—of course, he'd gaped. He had his mind on tomorrow. Walking in on a friend with most of her clothes off had made him understandably uncomfortable.

She shouldn't have snapped at him.

And she refused to feel hurt that he could not have cared less about getting an eyeful of her in her skimpy undies.

Because no matter what anybody said, Ella was not in love with Ian. No way.

"You get a chance to talk to Abby?" he asked.

"Yeah. Just briefly. She sends her love and she got an A on her math test."

"Like mother, like daughter."

She grinned. "Brains do run in the family."

"Ready?" he asked, his gaze warm on her. Sometimes he looked at her as though he liked what he saw.

But why wouldn't he? They were friends. He liked *her*.

And she needed to quit second-guessing his every random glance in her direction.

She nodded. "I'm starved."

He offered his arm, and she took it.

Round in structure, with a cone-shaped red-cedar ceiling, the dining room at the center of the Isabel Inn had the same feel as the rest of the hotel—casually elegant and cozy. Ella and Ian split a bottle of local wine and both chose Dungeness crab Caesar salad, with rack of lamb for the main course.

Ian kept the talk light and she went along with that, letting the evening serve as a distraction from any worries he might have about tomorrow. She didn't mention the Bravos and neither did he.

Outside, the sky remained layered in clouds, though the rain had stopped. After the meal, they detoured to the suite to get jackets. Leaving their shoes behind on the deck, they went down two sets of steps to the beach, where they strolled barefoot in the sand. The sun sent fingers of orange spreading over the sky as it slipped below the horizon way out there on the ocean.

"I could learn to like it here," she said as they stood side by side a few feet from the incoming waves, watching the sky slowly darken.

He made a sound of agreement low in his throat, his gaze on the horizon. "It's a good place to be a kid—safe," he said quietly. "Lots of time on the beach in the summers. We had a big house on a hill—Rhinehart Hill. And us kids had the run of it. A big backyard, with a swing set and tall trees all around. I remember my mom used to..." He blinked several times in rapid succession.

She didn't know what to say, what to do in this

moment. Beg him to go on? Pretend he hadn't said anything?

The memories he'd just shared sounded lovely. Nothing traumatic. A happy family in which the children felt safe and loved—but how horrible for a little boy to have been torn from his good life so completely, to find himself lost in a strange land, attacked and brutalized by a wild animal, waking up in a hospital where the people spoke words he didn't understand.

He was watching her now, his mouth set, his eyes impossible to read.

"Don't stop," she said hopefully. Now that he'd turned to her, it felt wrong not to encourage his good memories. "Your mom used to…?"

His brows cinched together. "Nah."

Please… She almost kept after him. But if he didn't want to go on about it, well, right now she felt wrong pushing him.

"Come on, let's go back." He offered his big hand. She looked down at it, a little bit stunned. Nine years she'd known this man, worked alongside him, called him her friend, trusted her daughter to his care on a regular basis.

And yet she couldn't recall ever holding his hand—not that it was a big deal, a little hand-holding. Between friends.

She slipped her fingers in his. His warm, strong grip felt good.

Maybe too good…

"Have you remembered a lot?" she asked.

He squeezed her fingers. "Enough." And he smiled, a rueful sort of smile that had her heart aching for him.

And she couldn't tell—did he mean that he'd remembered "enough"? Or that he'd said "enough" on the subject and didn't want to talk about it anymore?

Out across the water, the gulls cried to each other.

"Ell." With the hand that wasn't holding hers, he touched her cheek, the pad of his index finger catching a few windblown strands of hair, guiding them back behind the curve of her ear. She felt that touch like a brand, a line of heat seared into her skin. "In the past few weeks, I've remembered a lot about this town, about my family here. About my life here."

"A good life, you said…"

"It was, yeah."

"I'm…" Her throat clutched. She gave a sharp cough to clear it. "I'm glad."

"Hey…"

"Hmm?"

"You're not going to start bawling on me, are you?"

With a sniffle and a shake of her head, she blinked the moisture away. "Not a chance, McNeill."

"Good, then." Tugging on her hand, he turned for the hotel. "Let's go in."

In their suite, he said he had messages to catch up on. She probably ought to check her correspondence, too. Plus, it was almost nine now—meaning midnight in Manhattan.

She covered a yawn. "I think jet lag may be catching up with me." And they had a big day tomorrow.

"Breakfast in the dining room?"

"Done." She retreated to her room, where she stared at the turned-back bed and muttered to herself, "Forget work."

A few minutes later, in comfy sleep shorts and a worn T-shirt, she climbed between the covers and turned off the lamp.

Ella dreamed of Lake Thunderbird, in Norman, Oklahoma. In the dream, she was a little girl, still living in Norman with her parents, who adored her, in a small, one-story brick house. Her mom and dad loved their boat, the *Sweet Home*. Ella loved it, too.

In the dream, aboard the *Sweet Home*, they drifted on the shifting waters of the lake. Just the three of them, her mom in the galley, making sandwiches, her dad at the wheel. Her child self sat aft, watching clouds gather over the water, knowing that before long, the rain would start. Rain often brought thunder and lightning. Any minute now, her dad would turn the boat for the safety of the dock.

It was an old dream, a good dream. And most times, the dream stayed good and they made it safely to shore, the same as they always had in real life.

Well, except for that one time. The time the storm came so quickly, pouncing on them out of nowhere, like some wild animal, the sky cracking open with streaks of lightning and booms of angry thunder.

When it finally ended, there was dead calm. Ella floated in her lifejacket, completely alone, crying for her mom and dad and getting only silence in reply.

Tonight, the dream took the bad direction. Lightning lit up the sky, and her mother's voice cried to her, desperate and terrified...

She had no idea what woke her.

One moment she sat on the *Sweet Home* staring up as her mother screamed her name and lighting split the sky—the next her eyes popped open on her shadowed bedroom at the Isabel Inn. She lay there on her back, gazing up at the ceiling, straining her ears for the slightest sound.

Nothing.

She glanced at the blue numerals on the bedside clock—1:01 on Friday morning, and her mouth felt so dry.

Leaving the light off, she threw back the covers, swung her feet to the rug and padded to the bathroom. A glass of tap water later, she returned to the bed.

Before she could reach the comfort of the covers, she heard, faintly, a strangled sort of cry, followed by a rough shout of, "No!"

Ian's voice.

Had someone broken into the suite? Was Ian fighting off an attacker?

Her heart roared in her ears as her mind raced. Should she rush to help him however she could? Call the front desk?

And beyond her bedroom door now? Only silence. Her pulse roaring in her ears, she glanced around the dark room, looking for a makeshift weapon.

Seriously, where could a girl get a sturdy, column-style table lamp when she needed one? The two that flanked her bed had fat glass bases, so unwieldy for self-defense.

On tiptoe, her breath shuddering in and out, she crept to the door, carefully disengaged the lock and pulled it inward.

Dead quiet. In the slanting shafts of illumination from the deck and landscape lights outside, the living area sat silent—and apparently undisturbed.

She heard a low moan. It came from beyond the partway-open door to Ian's room. No sounds of a struggle, though.

On tiptoe, she crossed the living area and peeked in there, saw someone in the bed—Ian, no doubt. As she stared, he groaned again and turned over. She could see his face well enough then to note the signs of distress—eyebrows crunched together, mouth turned down.

So then. A nightmare.

She had them, too—in fact, she'd been having the nightmare she hated most when Ian's shout woke her.

As she debated whether to wake him, he rolled over again and then again. Tossing and turning, he moaned in protest at whatever was happening inside his head.

She couldn't just leave. "Ian…"

He moaned some more and then gruffly shouted, "No!" again.

"Ian, wake up. Ian!"

He just kept rolling around. And then he was kicking and punching. The covers couldn't hold him. He shoved them away. In nothing but a pair of boxer briefs, he went on wrestling with some invisible foe.

"Ian…" She approached the bed, all too aware that she risked getting punched or kicked in the face. "Ian, come on. You need to wake up." She bent too close and then made the mistake of touching the hard bulge of his shoulder.

In the blink of an eye, he grabbed her arm, yanked her down on top of him and then rolled her under him.

"Ian!" She shouted it right in his face.

"Ungh!" His head reared back.

She knew with absolute certainty that he would headbutt her. "Ian, stop!"

He flinched—and then, at last, his eyes blinked open. "What…? Ella?"

They stared at each other. She dared to draw a slow, shaky breath. "You were having a nightmare."

"I don't… My God, Ell. I'm sorry…" He rolled away.

They lay on their backs, side by side, panting as though they'd just run a marathon.

And then he reached over and turned on the

lamp. As she blinked against the sudden brightness, he flopped back on the pillow.

"You okay?" he asked after a moment.

She rolled her head his way. He had one muscular forearm thrown across his eyes. His big chest, glistening with a faint sheen of sweat and crisscrossed with the remnants of pale, faded scars from the long-ago bear attack, expanded and contracted with each heavy breath.

"I'm good. Although, for a minute there, I had zero doubt you would headbutt me."

He turned his face her way again. He looked so tired. "I don't think I would've. But what do I know? Ell. I mean it. I really am sorry."

"Hey." She gave him a smile and waited for the corners of that gorgeous mouth to tip up in answer. "No harm done." She should get up and go.

But she didn't.

He rolled toward her and tucked his hands under his head, the position so boyish, somehow.

She rolled to face him. "Your nightmare just now. Was it the bear attack?"

He punched at the pillow, getting it the way he wanted it, then laying his tousled head back down. His eyes were indigo, a starless night. "Yeah. But it's not a coherent sort of dream, just terror and random images. No logical sequence. Claws and teeth coming at me, blood on snow."

"How awful."

He seemed to be studying her face. Finally, he said, "I must've been loud, to wake you up all the way in your room."

"There was a shout or two. At first, I thought maybe someone had broken in and attacked you."

He watched her so closely, his gaze moving over her face with slow care. Such a beautiful man. And such a pity she couldn't let herself hope for more than friendship with him. He quirked an eyebrow. "You came to save me?"

That made her laugh. "Yeah. Clearly, I need to sign up for that self-defense class I keep meaning to take."

"You're amazing."

"So true."

His gaze held hers. He lifted his hand. Light as a breath, he touched her hair. "And so beautiful."

Her heartbeat had picked up again. It echoed in her ears. "What are you doing, Ian?"

He guided a hank of hair back over her shoulder. "Bad idea, huh?"

Agree with the man, she commanded herself. *Tell him not to be foolish. Tell him that yes, absolutely, it's a bad, bad idea.* But her mouth opened, and she heard herself say softly, intimately, "You never made a move before."

"You're too important to me." He traced a line

down the center of her nose, leaving a trail of longing, a sizzle of sweet heat.

And she needed to call him on his crap. "I'm too important, you just said."

"That's right. You are."

"And yet, tonight, you want to pretend that I'm not?"

His forehead crinkled with a frown. "Didn't I just say it's not wise?"

"But you're doing it, anyway."

His breathing changed, his dilated pupils sharpening, a muscle twitching at his jaw. "You're right. I'm messed up tonight and not thinking clearly. You need to get up and go."

She did no such thing. "Not yet."

He groaned. "Ell. Come on. You're killing me here."

"I need you to tell me why. Why tonight, of all nights, do you want to change the rules?"

"Ell…"

"Just tell me why, Ian. That's what I need to know."

He glared at her—but then, with a hard huff of breath, he gave it up. "Because I'm all screwed up over whatever's going to happen tomorrow. I don't know these people. And yet I'm supposed to call them my family."

"You're going to be fine," she promised, though she had no way to know that for certain.

"Right." He didn't sound one bit convinced. "But there's more."

"I'm not following. More of what?"

"More reasons to want you tonight."

Pleasure tingled through her, a shower of happy sparks. Was she a total fool? Apparently so.

He went on, "I can't stop remembering what happened before we went to dinner, when I barged in on you in your black thong and satin bra, looking all kinds of smoking hot…"

More sparks. And a fizzy-champagne feeling in her tummy, just to hear him say he'd seen her as a desirable woman—desirable enough that she tempted him to take chances with their longtime friendship, with their partnership at Patch&Pebble.

She shouldn't feel happy about that. Lying here bantering with him in this intimate way posed as much of a risk for her as it did for him.

She should rise from this bed and go back to her own room.

Instead, she did more of what she shouldn't do. She teased him, "Kind of did you in, huh, me in my little satin thong?"

"Definitely did me in." His voice was a low growl. "Now I know that about you, Ell."

"That I wear underwear?"

His index finger cradled her chin, and he used the pad of his thumb to brush back and forth across her lips, causing all manner of havoc, striking sparks in her belly, sending shivers skating over her skin. "Such a smart mouth on you. And no. Not that you wear underwear. It's that you're all smooth and willowy underneath your clothes. That you're Ell, my friend. My partner in the company. But you're also a beautiful woman. It's a side of you I never let myself see before. And tonight was a bad night—until I woke up and found you here in bed underneath me."

His eyes were so dark. Turbulent. Yearning. They echoed the feelings that churned down inside her. They made her burn for something she should never let happen.

So foolish, to consider staying right here in this bed with him, to imagine letting herself give in to temptation.

Having sex with Ian…

She had to be out of her mind to make that kind of mistake.

And yet, she did want it—want *him*.

So what if he would never love her? It was the middle of the night on the far side of the country. Just her and Ian.

In his bed.

Why shouldn't she give him tonight—why shouldn't she take tonight for herself?

He leaned in, until they shared her pillow and his forehead met hers. He smelled of sandalwood and clean sweat, and her longing went fathoms deep.

To hold him. Be with him. For this one night.

"Ell," he whispered, his breath warm against her skin. "You need to say it. You need to just tell me no, or…"

"What?"

"Or say yes."

Her body ached for him. But her one absolute rule just might save her from herself. "You have condoms?" She loved her daughter more than her life. But a second unplanned pregnancy—or a surprise STD, for that matter? Not going to happen. "I'm on the pill, but…"

"…no method is foolproof," he finished for her as he tipped up her chin again. Lightning forked through her. "Protection on all fronts. I demand that, too, which is why I always have condoms. After all, I might meet an incredibly sexy brunette in a black thong who shows up in my bedroom to save me from the demons inside my head."

So much for that excuse to back out. She shouldn't be so thrilled at his answer. "Good."

"One more thing."

"What now?" Had he come to his senses and changed his mind? If so, she should be grateful.

But she wouldn't be. Not in the least.

He said, "You need to promise you won't let this come between us—as friends and at work. You need to be sure. It's just for tonight. You know who I am, Ell. I'm not going to wake up tomorrow and be someone different. Something got broken in me before Glynis found me. I don't care for hook-ups with random women, so I date. But it never lasts, and I doubt it ever will. I get bored—or that's what I tell myself. It's not that, really. I shut down is what I do. I shut down and I just want whoever she is this time gone."

Say no. Get up. Get out of here. The voice of reason in her head just kept getting fainter.

He said, "I want you so bad right now, but I'm not going to change. Remember my history. I'm not that guy, not someone any woman ought to pin her hopes on."

She almost laughed. "You think I don't know you? Please. After all these years?"

"So you're saying…?"

"No worries. I get it." She did get it. It hurt. But the truth did that sometimes. "I agree. It would be tonight and only tonight. And then we go back to being Ian and Ella, good friends and colleagues."

"That's right." He waited. The silence echoed

until he prompted, "Say it, then. Plain and simple. Yes or no?"

Say no, she reminded herself once more. The risks to their longtime friendship and to their partnership at work were too great. She could not take the chance—but she wanted him, and he wanted her. And this moment between them would never come again.

"Yes."

Chapter Five

Ian rolled away from her and stood.

Hardly believing she'd decided to do this, Ella canted up on her elbow and watched his broad, sculpted back, his rock-hard buttocks beneath the boxer briefs, as he walked away from her. His open suitcase sat on the rack in the corner. She watched him bend to take the little packets from a pocket.

He came back to her, a portrait in male grace, his legs thick with muscle, dusted with dark gold hair, one powerful thigh scored with faded scars—claw marks. The large, clear bulge at the front of his briefs had her catching her upper lip between her teeth and slowly biting down on it.

Dropping three condoms on the nightstand, he eased the briefs over his hardness and stepped out of them, letting them fall to the rug by the bed. His erection, thick and long, in scale with the rest of his body, stood up proud and ready.

"You should see your eyes." His grin stretched slowly as he got on the bed with her. "Dark. Soft. Wide."

He stretched out beside her, his warm hand slipping under her hair to cradle her nape as he brought his mouth to hers.

A kiss. Their first ever. Who knew this could happen?

Her own breathy moan echoed in her head as his lips worked their dark magic. Every inch of her softened. Her heart beat a hungry, deep rhythm and moisture gathered between her legs, wetting the cotton crotch of her sleep shorts.

With one hand, he fisted her hair as he held her in place for his mouth. With the other, he touched her, his fingers brushing her throat, closing on it, and then skating downward, over her collarbones and the top of her chest, between her breasts. Her pulse pounded harder as his palm lingered there. Could he feel her heart, the way it beat so hard and deep?

His hand glided lower as he kept on kissing her. He took her tongue, sucking it into the warm cave of his mouth, sliding his around it, groaning low as he tasted her. She moaned in answer.

And then he cupped a breast through her T-shirt, squeezing it hard enough to create a thrilling ache, one that skirted deliciously close to pain—so good. So right. He caught her hard nipple between his thumb and forefinger, pinching it, rolling it. She lifted her chest for him, moaning, eager for more.

His hand skated on down, taking the hem of her shirt, yanking it up, baring her breasts so he could fondle them with nothing in the way as he guided her over onto her back. Letting go of her mouth, he covered a breast, sucking it past his lips, flicking the nipple with his tongue until she was panting his name, holding him hard and tight against her.

She said things, encouraging things, needful things, punctuating them with "Yes," followed by "Oh, please…"

He pulled away. Her eyes fluttered open. His were midnight blue, full of magic and heat.

"Lift your arms."

She obeyed. Grabbing the shirt now wadded up above her breasts, he yanked it higher, over her face. The crewneck caught on her chin. She giggled. But then he gave another tug and off it came.

He tossed it over his shoulder. "There you are." He smiled at her—an intent, predatory sort of smile.

And then he took her mouth again. She kissed him back, a kiss so deep, their tongues twining together, so hungry and wild.

His fingers ventured lower. He slipped them under the waistband of her sleep shorts, touching her intimately.

It felt so good. She let out a pleasured cry.

"You're so wet, Ell. Wet for me…" His low growl of approval echoed in her head as he went on kissing her endlessly, his fingers sliding in her wetness, entering her, pulling out to rub along her eager sex and then to push at her shorts.

"Off," he muttered. "Out of the way…"

She helped him push the shorts down, kicking them off with one foot as she shoved at them with the other.

"Naked," he said, the word a dark promise whispered into her open mouth. "So good. You feel so good…" His fingers opened her, filled her—one and then another and then a third finger, too.

And then he was rolling, pulling her over him to straddle him, getting hold of her bottom with both big hands and guiding her up to her knees.

"Headboard," he commanded.

Tufted and bolted to the wall, the headboard seemed a bad bet for bracing herself. Still, she managed to grab the top of it and slip her fingers in behind it enough that she could hold on tight.

He pulled her throbbing center down onto his face.

Oh. My. Goodness. Ian knew what to do with that perfect mouth of his. He buried his tongue in her, used his chin and even his teeth. She threw back her head and screamed at the ceiling.

"Be good, Ell," he chided from down between her legs. "Someone will sic the manager on us…"

"Okay," she panted. "I will…" The rest was nothing but nonsense syllables as he feasted on her like a starving man at a royal banquet.

It didn't take long. She lit up like a string of firecrackers on the Fourth of July, biting her lip to hold her cries of ecstasy to a reasonable volume. Really, she'd had no idea that a climax he'd so quickly stirred could last such a very long time.

Hers went on and on, and he stayed with her through it, somehow knowing when to ease off and when to latch on tight again.

When the last spark had faded and there was only a shimmer and a quiver and a glow, she sank to her butt on his chest with a long sigh.

He grinned up at her, his face wet from cheek to chin from what he'd done to her. "Ell. Look at you. Flushed and satisfied, hair all over the place, breathing so hard. It's a good look. A great look. Get down here." He rearranged her on top of him, lifting her hips and guiding them lower, so she straddled him, his erection tucked against her sex, her upper body on his chest.

"You're a mess," she said, laughing, sliding her butt onto his washboard stomach, sitting up again. Grabbing her T-shirt, which had somehow ended up right there beside them on the bed, she wadded it up and wiped his face with it.

He licked his lips. "Delicious."

"Yeah, well." She pitched the T-shirt over the side of the bed. "The receiving end was nothing short of spectacular."

He reached up with both hands, pulling her closer. Forking his fingers into her hair at either temple, he combed through the long strands and then wrapped a big hank of it around his right palm. "Come down here." His gravelly voice sent heat streaking along every nerve ending. "Not done with you yet. Not by a long shot." He pulled her down.

Their lips met.

And it started all over again.

His hands touched her everywhere. His skilled mouth conjured more magic. When he rose above her and reached for a condom, she stared up into those beautiful eyes of his and wondered how they'd gotten here—the two of them, after all these years, in bed together, eager and naked, no holds barred.

He rolled the condom down his thick length.

"Ell," he said as he covered her.

"Yes, Ian. Now…" She wrapped her arms and legs around him good and tight.

He came into her in one hard, hungry thrust, stretching her open, big enough to hurt her—but in the best sense of the word. She groaned at the feel of him as he started to move.

Whatever happened, whatever tonight did to them, to what they'd built together in the past nine years, so be it. Right now, joined to him in the most elemental way, she had zero regrets. He kissed her, deep and long and perfectly, as their bodies moved together, hard and fast and hungry.

Her climax barreled toward her—until he slowed down.

Groaning in protest, she slapped at his arm, grabbing on, digging her nails in a little. "I was almost there…"

"Patience." He gave a low laugh and bit the side of her neck as he kept right on moving, taking his time, pulling all the way out until she knew she would lose him—but then sliding right back in, so slow and so deep, like waves in the ocean, a rolling, endless internal caress.

Again, she rose toward the peak, a slower, more thrilling, all-encompassing rise. The pulse of her arousal expanded through her. Her body flared and burned, the pleasure molten, all-encompassing.

And then she was coming, a shudder rippling all through her, across her skin and deeper, down into her bones. It lasted so long, flaring and then flagging, only to start again, climbing higher than before.

As she hit the peak, he rolled them, taking the bottom position, grabbing her hips and yanking her down onto him, getting deeper than ever, though that hardly seemed possible.

When she collapsed on top of him, he rolled again, claiming the dominant position once more. She held on, staring up at him, dazed and so satisfied, as he drove in for the last time and threw his head back with a groan that seemed to come from the very core of him.

When she woke, she felt disoriented at first and didn't know where she was.

Warm, strong arms held her. She felt safe. Cared for.

Slowly, she opened her eyes.

It all came back.

Ian's arms. Ian's bed. He'd had a nightmare and she came to check on him. Things got interesting from there.

It felt so good, being held by him. He smelled

cool and dark, like deep woods. Peering through the dimness at his sleeping face, she grinned.

Sex with Ian. Amazing.

And it must be late.

She snuggled in again and shut her eyes, but sleep didn't come.

As the seconds ticked by, she grew uncomfortable. After all, they'd agreed on just this one night. It seemed safer, wiser, to get out of here before he woke.

She stirred and pushed gently at his warm, rock-hard chest. At first, he didn't budge. But when she pushed a second time, he rolled onto his back.

Carefully, so as not to wake him, she slid out from under the blankets and eased her feet to the rug. She got lucky and found her sleep shorts and wrinkled tee in a wad a few inches from her toes.

Scooping them up, she headed for the door, which stood open on the central room. Slipping through, she silently pulled the door shut behind her.

When she emerged from her room at eight the next morning, Ian sat on the sofa with his laptop open on the coffee table in front of him. Dressed in tan pants and a dark blue shirt, he looked so handsome it made her heart hurt. Glancing up, he smiled at her, a warm, gorgeous smile that caused an ache in her solar plexus—desire, apprehension and a wave of sadness, all mixed up together.

"Ready?" she asked, forcing her lips to lift at the corners.

He shut the laptop and rose. "Lead on."

She grabbed her shoulder bag, and they went to the dining room.

"You seem quiet," she remarked—quietly—once the server had poured them coffee and left them alone.

"Big day," he replied.

Her mouth felt dry. She sipped her coffee, hated how uncomfortable she felt and wondered if she should bring up the elephant at the table or if maybe he would.

Oh, God. Would they just sit here, eating their salmon eggs Benedict, pretending that nothing had happened last night?

She sipped more coffee. "It's good," she said, and it was. Hand roasted locally using the highest quality coffee beans, their server had told them.

He sipped, too, and made a low sound of agreement.

Ugh. She and Ian had never had a shortage of things to say to each other. Until now.

Last night had been amazing. But this?

Awkward didn't begin to cover it.

She did what people do when they don't know what to say—focused on her surroundings.

The dining room had windows all around. She stared out at the overcast morning, at the endless expanse of ocean beyond the mist-shrouded beach.

Another couple sat at the next table over—young, early twenties at most. The guy had full sleeves of ink down both lean arms. The girl wore her pink hair in a pixie cut. She had piercings in her nose and lower lip.

The two sat side by side, whispering to each other. A romantic trip to the coast, no doubt. The guy pulled the girl closer, and they shared a slow kiss. When they took a break from their PDA to sip coffee, they kept their bodies canted toward each other, shoulders touching.

Watching them made her wistful. To be that young and that much in love…

She heard the clink of Ian's cup against his saucer and shifted her glance to him as he leaned toward her across the snow-white tablecloth. "Looks like those two had a good night."

"Young love. Nothing like it."

His gaze held hers. "Maybe. Speaking just for myself, though, I had a *great* night." He said it softly. Intimately. Her sad feelings evaporated, and her heart seemed to expand with sheer happiness. And he wasn't finished. "It started out bad. But then you came in to save me, and everything got exponentially better."

She reminded herself not to get carried away here. They'd had sex. He'd enjoyed it a lot. So had she. End of story. "Wow. Exponentially, huh?"

He gave her a slow nod, his gaze holding hers captive as he asked gruffly, "Did some idiot say it would just be one night?"

"That's right." Somehow, she kept her voice cool, relaxed. "Sure was great while it lasted."

Their server appeared with the food. She chattered about wild-caught coho salmon and house-baked English muffins. A moment after she left, she came zipping right back to refill their coffee cups.

"What else can I bring you?" she chirped.

"We're good for now," Ian replied.

"All right then. I'll leave you to it." And finally, she did.

The minute she trotted off, Ian said, "We're here for three more nights." He took a bite of eggs, salmon and muffin. After he swallowed, he set down his fork. "Be a shame to waste them."

Three more nights. She couldn't wait.

Did that make her a fool? When this trip ended, then what?

Wrong questions, she chided herself. She wanted him, and he'd made it thrillingly clear he wanted her right back. They had three nights, just the two of them, on the far side of America, sharing the same suite. Why not make the most of it? For tonight and the two nights that followed, she would do something just for the sheer pleasure it brought.

And the future could damn well look after itself.

"Ell."

"Hmm?"

"Will you consider it?" Dear Lord, the way he looked at her—both tender and tentative.

Yes, she thought. She answered more carefully, "Yes. I will, um, consider it."

One bronze eyebrow lifted. She knew he would press her for a definite answer. But in the end, he only gave her a slow, panty-melting smile and said, "A man can't ask for more."

They ate in silence for a bit. The food was excellent, and now she had tonight to look forward to.

Maybe.

If she didn't get cold feet. If *he* didn't suddenly remember all the reasons having her in his bed could mess with their friendship and screw up their professional relationship.

Right now, they needed to focus on the reason they'd come to Oregon.

Ian had something important to do.

She dared to ask again, "Are you going to call one of your brothers?"

"No need."

She opened her mouth to object.

He went on before she got a word out, "There's a family business a few miles outside town, Valentine Logging. It's on the docks in Warrenton, a short drive from here. Two of my brothers, Daniel and Connor, run the place. We'll head up there after breakfast."

Ian tried to think about good things—like Ella, naked.

Ella naked was the best thing that had happened to him in a long time. He wanted to see her that way again—the sooner the better. Tonight, definitely.

No, she hadn't exactly said yes to that. Yet. But he intended to be at his most convincing once he had her alone in the suite again.

No, he'd never in his wildest dreams planned to put a move on her. He'd meant it when he said she mattered too much to him to take that kind of chance with what they had together.

However, too late now.

He'd blown it. The result had been fantastic—which meant he couldn't wait to blow it again. They had three days left here at the Isabel Inn. He wanted to spend every moment of today and Saturday and Sunday alone with Ella in their suite.

Unfortunately, they hadn't come all the way to Oregon so that he could get Ella into bed.

They'd come so that he could meet the Bravos.

He felt he *should* meet the Bravos.

But did he *want* to meet the Bravos?

Hell, no.

He just wanted to take Ella back to the suite and make love to her all day.

Failing that, he longed to toss their suitcases in the rental car and head for Portland. He could call Audrey on the way, tell her to find them a flight that would get them out of Oregon, stat.

Ella watched him too closely—the way she always did. "Breathe," she said gently. "It's going to be fine."

Of course it was. No big deal. Meet the long-lost family. Piece of cake.

The cheerful waitress brought the bill. He added a large tip and charged it to the room.

Too soon after that, he and Ella climbed in the rented SUV and headed for Warrenton. The drive up the coast took a mere twenty minutes.

The morning mist had burned off, and the sun shone bright when he pulled the Lexus to a stop in front of a barnlike building with a long porch in front, steps going up on either side and a sign above the entrance: Valentine Logging.

Ella said something, but his mind was spinning and he didn't really hear her actual words.

He answered with a nod and, "Let's do this," as he yanked the handle to open his door.

After that, everything had a dreamlike quality to it. In a dream, with Ella at his side, he floated up the wooden stairs, across the deck-like porch and through the door that led into Valentine Logging.

They entered a front office. Nothing fancy— some guest chairs, a table, a middle-aged woman with a kind face behind a desk near an inner door.

The woman rose. "Hey. I'm Midge. What can I do for you?"

"I would like to speak with Daniel Bravo."

"Sure. D'you have an appointment?"

"I don't, no."

"Fair enough. Just give me your name, then, and why you're here."

His throat felt tight. He coughed into his hand to clear it. "I'm Ian McNeill. As to why…" Words completely failed him. He stood there with his mouth half-open and no idea how to go on.

This shouldn't be all that difficult. What was wrong with him? He needed to snap out of it.

Ella came to his rescue. "It's a personal matter concerning the Bravo family."

He'd been grateful for Ella more than once in his life—but never as grateful as right now. Somehow, he managed to shut his mouth. Ella brushed a hand down his arm, a touch meant to reassure. He grabbed her fingers, wove his between them and held on good and tight.

Midge said, "Just have a seat. I'll be right back." She disappeared into the hallway beyond the inner door.

Ella squeezed his hand. "Holding up okay?"

He made a sound—a scoff with a side of absolute terror. "Don't get on me for not calling first."

"Me, get on you? Never."

"Ha. Right."

Midge returned. "Come on back."

He was glad he hadn't sat down. At this moment, he doubted he could have made his rubbery legs take him from sitting to upright. Stiffly, holding on to Ella for dear life, he followed Midge into the hallway. Halfway along on the right, a door stood open.

"Here you go." With a bright smile and a firm nod, Midge turned and headed back the way they'd come.

"Come on in," a man said from inside. Ian caught his first glimpse of the man. Dirty-blond hair, blue eyes—a paler blue than Ian's. Square jaw, broad shoulders. He could be Ian's brother.

Because he was.

Ian pulled his hand from Ella's and guided her in ahead of him. As usual, she understood. He needed her to speak first.

Like the reception area out front, Daniel Bravo's office was simple. Functional. A sitting area, a large desk, a window behind the desk with a view of the Columbia River. Ian took it all in before making himself look at Daniel again.

"I'm Daniel Bravo," he said to Ella and offered his hand.

Ella shook it, gave Daniel her name and stepped aside. "This is Ian McNeill."

"Ian." Daniel seemed nonplussed, but he played along, offering his hand. "Hey."

Ian reached out and took it. They shook and let go. He needed to speak. No more putting it off. He opened his mouth. Hallelujah! Words came out. "I'm, um, finding I don't know exactly how to do this."

Daniel frowned, a look of concern. "Are you all right?"

"Not really…"

"Have a seat." He gestured at the sofa and chairs to Ian's left.

"Uh, no. No sitting. Not yet."

Daniel seemed at a loss as to how to reply to that. "Well. All right. Is there anything I can—"

"No," Ian cut him off, raising a hand, palm out. "Wait."

Daniel cleared his throat. "Okay…"

Ian pushed more words out. "Eighteen years ago, I was adopted from a Russian orphanage by a woman named Glynis McNeill. I was believed to be about ten when Glynis adopted me. At the time, I had no memory of my early life. She took me back to America, gave me her name and brought me up as her own."

From about the moment that Ian had said the word *Russian*, Daniel's face changed. His eyes went blank, a distant, glacial blue. The warm color leached from his tan skin. "Finn. Oh, my God. Finn?" He reached out.

Ian blinked. Was he getting a hug? *Not ready for that.* But his reflexes were nonexistent.

Daniel Bravo wrapped him in thick lumberjack arms. "I knew it," he whispered, the words sandpaper-rough in Ian's ear. "There was something about you. When you walked in here, I knew you." He took Ian by the arms and stood back. "Alive. By God. Alive all this time—Connor! Connor, get in here!"

Ian blinked at him. This all felt…impossible. Unreal. Bizarre.

Another man, clearly a brother, came and stood in the doorway. "What? Did somebody die?" He had darker hair and a leaner build than either Daniel or Ian, but still, the family resemblance was unmistakable.

"I… I've brought proof," Ian heard himself announce, and he whipped out a memory stick. "It's on here. I've been remembering, lately. I hired an investigator. He compiled an extensive file." He shoved it at Daniel, who stared at it, not taking it, until Ian added, "Just, you know, give it a look whenever you're ready."

"Yeah, okay. Will do." With a numb sort of nod, Daniel took it and stuck it in his pants pocket.

Still in the doorway, Connor Bravo asked Daniel, "What's going on?" Daniel glanced at his brother—well, more like stared, glassy-eyed. "Daniel," Connor demanded, "what the hell just happened?"

"It's Finn, damn it," growled Daniel. "Connor, just look at him. It's Finn…"

Connor's gaze swung to Ian. He stared, looking sucker punched. "Finn? What the…?" And then he swore under his breath. "Right. I see it. Finn. My God."

A few seconds later, Ian found himself submitting to a second brotherly embrace. Connor clapped him on the back, exclaiming, "Damn it. I can't believe it. But you're right, Daniel. Just seeing his face, you can tell. It's so obvious…"

When Connor finally let him go, Ian turned to find Ella. She stepped right up and took his arm. He clapped a hand over hers so she couldn't get away.

Connor said, "Come on, sit over here."

Moving in a living dream, he went where Ella guided him. Taking one end of the sofa, he pulled her down to sit by him, good and close so he could grab her, keep her from going if she tried to get up without him.

Daniel offered scotch. It wasn't even ten in the morning, but he and Connor nodded. Only Ella took a pass.

For a while, they talked. It was almost bearable. He gave them the short version of his life so far, explaining a little more about his adoptive mother and the company he'd inherited from her. He spoke of the bear attack all those years ago, and how he still had no idea how he'd traveled all the way from where he'd wandered off near Irkutsk to the hospital in Krasnoyarsk. They agreed on DNA tests. An ancient uncle named Percy Valentine, whom Ian vaguely recalled from the memories he was slowly reclaiming and from the PI's report, would arrange those. Percy had been the one in charge of the search for him over the last twenty years. Connor and Daniel spoke in hushed tones about that.

"It's doubtful, then, that we ever would have

found you," said Daniel, looking grim. "The search for you was extensive, but I don't think it ranged as far away as you ended up."

He explained about his refusal to talk until after Glynis had brought him safely to New York. "I don't think anyone in the hospital or the orphanage where they sent me knew I was American. There were a lot of kids in that orphanage. None of the staff had the time to coax information from some messed-up, scarred kid who didn't talk."

Ian counted the minutes until he and Ella could go. His brothers seemed like good men, but his brain was on overload. He needed to get out, get some space. Process this crap.

Connor asked how long he and Ella had been together.

Ella took that on with an easy smile. "We've been friends since Glynis hired me as an intern at Patch&Pebble. That was nine years ago now."

"Ah," said Connor, apparently readjusting his view of her from romantic interest to good friend.

When Ian, pulling Ella up with him, rose to go, Daniel put up a hand. "Hold on. We need phone numbers and an address, so we can reach you."

"It's all on that stick I gave you."

"Great," said Connor. "But humor us." He whipped out a phone. "Both of you. Send yourselves a text." Unlocking the device, he handed it to Ian.

Ian sent the message. His own phone chimed in his pocket. He passed Connor's phone to Ella, and she did the same.

Daniel laughed. "Thank you. Now, no matter what happens, we know how to reach you. Where are you staying?"

"The Isabel Inn."

"Good choice." Connor clearly approved. "How long do we have you here in town?"

Have him? What did that mean? How much time would they expect him to spend with them, hanging out with them or whatever?

Yeah, he knew that he'd be called on to meet the rest of the Bravos, but right now all he could think about was getting away, decompressing, finding his way past the unreality of having brothers and sisters, a whole family lost to him completely since he was eight—both physically and inside his head.

Ella prompted, "Ian…"

He remembered he was supposed to answer Connor's question. "We're flying back to New York on Monday."

Daniel let out a relieved-sounding sigh. "Good. At least we have a few days to get to know you a little."

Connor said, "Starting tonight."

"Right," Daniel agreed. "Any chance you remember the house where you lived before the ill-fated trip to Russia?"

"I do... On a hill, forest all around, a big backyard, grass and swings, a jungle gym. People in town called it the Bravo house."

"That's it," said Daniel. "I still live in that same house on Rhinehart Hill with my wife and kids. And I'm calling a family dinner tonight. You can see the rest of your brothers and sisters. They're not going to believe it, that you're here at last."

Connor added, "And Aunt Daffy and Uncle Percy are well into their eighties now."

Daniel nodded. "We'll have to take special care telling them, break the news gently."

"Yeah," Connor said. "It's a good shock, but a shock nonetheless."

Daniel nodded again. "I'm betting we can get everyone up at the house for this..."

"No doubt," Connor agreed. "You couldn't keep them away if you tried." He turned to Ian. "Plus, when Daniel calls a family dinner, everybody shows. That's how he brought us up after Mom and Dad died—attendance required at dinner every Sunday *and* any night Daniel decided we all ought to be there. He was a pain in the ass as a father figure."

"I raised you up right." Daniel said it with pride.

"Harper lives in Portland now, but I'm guessing she'll get here no matter what." Ian remembered Harper, eighth born, as a blonde sprite of five or so. She and Hailey, born ten months before her, had been inseparable. Daniel went on, "And right now, luck's with us and Madison's in town."

Ian had no memory of anyone named Madison in the family. "I don't remember a Madison."

Daniel laughed. "That's another long story. Madison Delaney was born Aislinn. The two were switched shortly after birth."

"Hold on," said Ian. "Madison *Delaney*, you said, like the actress?"

"Not *like* the actress. Madison *is* the actress." Daniel beamed with brotherly pride. "That's right, our sister is a bona fide movie star. But don't tell anyone. It's a family secret. Madison likes her privacy."

"Uh, so what you're saying is that Madison is genetically a Bravo and that the Aislinn *I* remember…"

"…is our sister, same as always. Just not by blood. It's a mind-bender, I know. And a great story, but one for another time."

Connor had his phone out again. Both Ian's and Ella's phones chimed. "I just sent you both Daniel's address and phone number." Ian already had them.

But before he could say so, Daniel announced,

"Let's say six thirty. Up at my house, the Bravo house."

Connor put in, "We'll get everyone together—wives, husbands, fiancés and kids included. Uncle Percy and Aunt Daffy, too."

"Just come." Daniel clapped him on the shoulder. "I know this has to be seriously overwhelming. But you'll get used to us." Daniel's eyes were wet. He blinked the moisture away and aimed a giant smile at Ian. "Man, I cannot tell you. I always believed this would happen, but sometimes I doubted."

"We all did," Connor said gruffly.

"But now you're here. It's real," said Daniel. "And it's so damn good to have you home at last."

Chapter Six

Ella walked out of Valentine Logging with Ian clutching her hand so hard, she almost feared he would snap a bone.

He let her go so they could get into the Lexus.

She hooked her seat belt and gasped when he backed out fast from the space, slamming into Drive and speeding out of the graveled lot like something really bad chased after them.

"Are you okay?"

"Fine." Staring hard out the windshield, he hit the gas, his mouth a hard line.

"Ian, come on. You are not fine."

Dead silence from his side of the car—and

when he turned onto the Coast Highway, he went even faster.

"Ian, you're going to get a ticket if you don't slow down."

He sent her a seething look, but at least he put his foot on the brake and slowed to the speed limit.

"Are we going back to the hotel?" she asked.

For that, he granted her a sharp nod and a gruff, "That's right."

She gave up and let the rest of the ride go by in silence.

At the inn, he parked in the lot and got out so fast, she wondered if maybe his seat had caught fire. He headed straight for the lobby and from there to the suite. She followed, kind of wishing she had somewhere else to go.

In their room, he shut the door too hard and turned to her. "I'm sorry," he said through clenched teeth.

She stared up into his haunted eyes. The visit to Valentine Logging had thrilled his long-lost brothers. Ian, though? Not so much. "Are you going to talk to me?"

He took her by the upper arms in a too-firm grip. She couldn't decide if he thought she needed steadying—or he was holding on for dear life. "I can't do this."

"You just did. I know it wasn't easy for you. But objectively, it went great."

"Objectively?" he snarled. "Ella, what does that even mean?"

"It means that your brothers were so happy to see you, that the rest of the family can't wait to get to know you, that they seemed to me like good people, the kind of men who'll have your back no matter what happens. It means you didn't lose your only family when Glynis died. You've got a bunch of brothers and sisters who never gave up on finding you someday—not to mention an ancient great-aunt and great-uncle who've been searching for you all this time." What she wouldn't give to suddenly discover she had a big, loving family somewhere in this world, a family that couldn't wait to meet her, to bring her into the fold.

Ian refused to see the situation the way she did. He muttered, "I don't know these people. They're like ghosts to me, vague memories, more and more of them, all this stuff coming back to me, filling up my head. I remember them all, but mostly, those memories feel like they belong to someone else."

When they got home to New York, she would start working on him to see his old therapist or find someone new to talk to. But right now, she needed to figure out a way to settle the man down.

"I need to go," he said.

"Go where?"

"Home." He released her and headed for his bedroom. "Pack," he said over his shoulder. "I'll call Audrey on the way to Portland. She can get us a flight."

Ella remained by the door where he'd left her as she tried to decide what to do next. He would regret running away, but outright resistance at this juncture would be futile.

She could hear him in the bedroom, pacing, see him each time he went by the open door—from the bathroom to his suitcase, to the chair in the corner—gathering up his things, stuffing them in the bag.

Slowly, she approached the doorway to his room. When she got there, she leaned against the door frame.

He glanced up from his suitcase and scowled at her. "What'd I say? Come on, Ell. You need to pack."

She gave him a smile—a serene one, she hoped. "I will."

"Well, then…?"

"First, though, I think we could both use a nice walk on the beach."

His scowl deepened. "Don't try to redirect my attention. We're going. As soon as possible. You need to pack."

"I get it." She held out her hand. "A walk on the beach. Please?"

For a moment, she knew she'd lose him. He'd return to his frantic packing.

But then he let out a slow breath and grumbled, "I know what you're doing."

She kept her hand out and waited, holding his unhappy gaze.

Finally, he came to her, took the hand she offered, guided it behind her and pulled her in close.

With a sigh of relief, she let her head rest on his hard chest.

His free hand touched her hair at the crown of her head. Skimming a finger down over her cheek, he lifted her chin. "I don't deserve a friend like you."

"Hmm. You have a valid point. Because yeah. I'm pretty great—and you, my friend, need your feet in the sand."

They used the set of wooden stairs off the back deck and then took the second, longer set down to the beach.

It was a little before eleven, and the sky had cleared to a powder blue. They took off their shoes, rolled their cuffs and walked to the water's edge, where they turned and walked south, their footprints shining in the wet sand, vanishing as the fingers of each wave slid in and rolled away. After they'd gone maybe half a mile, Ella thought he seemed calmer.

Up ahead, a little girl and a boy who looked a bit older built a lopsided sandcastle twenty feet from the water. Ian took Ella's hand and led her closer to where the children squatted over their creation, patting at sand, the girl with her own small hands, the boy with a bright-colored shovel.

"I should call Abby," he said.

She nodded. "About four thirty's a good time, that's seven thirty there. She'll be home at her dad's. They should be done with dinner by then."

He tugged on her hand and they continued down the beach until they reached a headland where erosion had created a row of sea stacks marching down to the water's edge. One of the stacks not far from the waterline made a bench-like seat. They dropped their shoes in the sand, perched on the stack side by side and stared out over the constantly shifting water.

"I keep thinking I can't do this," he said, his eyes on the horizon.

"That's natural."

"It doesn't *feel* natural."

"So maybe *natural* was the wrong word. I'm guessing it's overwhelming for you. I mean, I feel kind of overwhelmed myself, and it's not even my family. But you didn't come all this way *not* to meet them."

"Do there *have* to be so many of them, though?"

She leaned his way and nudged him with her shoulder. "You're going to get through this. And once you do, you'll be glad you stuck it out."

He put his arm around her. She rested her head on his shoulder.

"Thanks, Ell, for coming with." She felt his breath against her hair and thrilled to the gentle pressure of his lips on the top of her head.

We're friends, she reminded herself.

Friends, and she needed to remember that. Friendship and great sex, nothing more going on here.

A half hour later, they climbed the stairs to the deck off the living area of their suite. A faucet by the glass door had a short hose attached to it. They rinsed their sandy feet before they went inside.

The moment she shut the door, he pulled her close.

Her shoes hit the floor and his followed right after as his beautiful mouth came down on hers. She gave herself up to it—to his kiss, to his big arms holding her so hard and tight.

When he lifted his head, she teased, "I'm not having sex with you unless you promise we're going up to your brother's house for dinner tonight and we're not leaving Oregon until Monday, as planned."

"That's blackmail." He dipped his head and caught her lower lip between his teeth, biting down just enough to make her moan.

Carefully, she pulled back to look in his eyes. "That hurt."

"You didn't *sound* hurt."

"Okay, fine. It was a good kind of hurt—and as for your blackmail remark, it's not blackmail if it's for your own good."

He tried to pull her close again.

She braced her palms against his rock-hard pecs and resisted. "Say yes. Say we'll go to dinner at Daniel's tonight and we'll stay in Oregon until Monday."

"How come you're so pushy? And why have you always been that way?"

"I get things done." She put a hand to her ear. "And that didn't exactly sound like a yes."

He grumbled, "Like I said, pushy."

"I'll be right here with you. All the way. Promise."

"Damn right you will."

"Say it, Ian."

"Yes." He growled the word and framed her face between his big, warm hands. She breathed in the scent of him—sandalwood, with a hint of the ocean after their walk. And man. All man. "And you bet your gorgeous ass you'll be here with me. There's no way I'm getting through this without you. Now kiss me and let me take you to bed. I need to work off some tension, and I need to do that with you."

"Whatever you want, Ian."

"Say that without smirking, Ella."

Lifting on her bare toes, she wrapped her hand around his nape and yanked him down for a kiss.

In his bed, an hour later, after he'd done all manner of wonderful things to her very willing naked body, he canted up on an elbow and lazily combed his fingers through her hair, spreading it out on the white pillow in a dark, wavy fan. "I think I've got a thing for your hair." He picked up a lock and brought it to his face. "Smells like coconut."

"It's called shampoo."

He chuckled, bent close and whispered in her ear, "Your stomach just growled."

"Yeah, 'cause you keep having sex with me instead of getting me some lunch."

"We can have a picnic basket sent over from the dining room."

"Ah. I like it. A picnic lunch in bed."

"Done." He braced up on an elbow, reached

across her for the hotel phone and called room service. When he hung up, he gazed down at her so tenderly. "Food will arrive at the door in about twenty minutes. We should hurry."

"Hurry to do what?"

"Here. Let me show you…" His mouth met hers as he peeled back the covers.

Nineteen minutes later when the food arrived, she was just catching her breath.

"Don't move from this bed," he commanded.

"Not a problem." She pushed her tangled hair out of her eyes and pulled the sheet up to cover her bare breasts.

As for Ian, he got up, pulled on his pants and headed for the living area.

Their picnic was fun. They sat on the tangled bed and ate sandwiches on freshly baked sourdough bread with chips and pickles—and chocolate chip cookies for dessert.

Ian really liked the cookies, so much so that he distracted her with a kiss as he snatched one of hers.

They wrestled for it, which meant cookie crumbs got everywhere.

They made love again, anyway.

At four thirty, he grabbed his phone and called Abby. Ella lay back on the crumb-strewn sheets and listened to him talking with her daughter, acting like the second dad everyone always accused him of being.

He laughed at something Abby had said—and it happened. Right then, something twisted inside her at the full, easy sound of that laugh.

Ella tried to throw up an internal wall of denial.

But it didn't really work.

It seemed more and more possible that Ian's bitchy ex-girlfriend had gotten it right: Ella loved Ian.

And not just as her very good friend.

He caught her eye and winked at her as Abby said something on the other end of the call.

How could she have let this happen?

More important—how could she make it stop?

Not by continuing to fall into bed with him, that was for sure.

Would that help, though, to call a halt to this while-we're-in-Oregon sexfest they'd decided to indulge in?

No! cried her foolish heart.

Because who cared if it would help her get over him? She didn't want to call a halt to this magic between them. She wanted every moment in his bed that she could get.

She wanted to play this out to the inevitable end, the one he'd warned her about last night. The end where he got bored, shut down and wanted her gone.

He watched her as he talked to Abby, sudden questions in his eyes. Had he seen something in her expression that worried him? He tipped his head to the side, mouthed, "You okay?"

She remembered—he'd winked at her, hadn't he?

With a grin, she winked back.

His expression relaxed. Now she envied him his absolute belief that he would never fall for anyone, that his heart was locked up tight, safe from breaking.

Silently, she called herself all kinds of fool.

Crap on a cracker. No question about it. She teetered on the edge with him. Maybe she hadn't quite fallen in love with him.

Or maybe she just refused to admit it had already happened.

But somehow, it all felt inevitable now. One more step.

And over she would go…

Chapter Seven

The Bravo house, a gorgeous three-story Colonial built at the turn of the twentieth century, stood above a wide, green sweep of lawn. The long, deep front porch invited everyone, guests and family alike, to have a seat, get comfortable, enjoy a tall iced tea on a hot day or maybe some cocoa on a cold winter's night.

Ian recognized the house immediately. It looked very much as it had in his newly recovered memories of the place—from the outside, anyway. Inside, many of the rooms had been updated, with a now-modern kitchen and new fixtures throughout.

When he and Ella arrived, the place was already

packed with his newfound family. Everywhere he turned, another familiar face smiled at him, most of them with blue eyes full of hope and joy.

They surrounded him. He thought he would suffocate under the force of their sheer happiness at the sight of him. As soon as he finished dealing with one of them, a new one came at him. He hugged them all.

Strangely, he found he recognized them, though most of them had yet to reach their teen years when he wandered off that snowy path near Irkutsk, never to see any of them again. Until now— on this cool, clear evening in May, two decades later, when they were all grown up, with husbands and wives and kids of their own.

Even Gracie, the baby of the family, four years old when he'd disappeared, had grown into a gorgeous young woman with an infectious laugh. His youngest sister had a job teaching history at Valentine Bay High and a fiancé she clearly adored. When she got married in June, she would have twin stepdaughters, too. Gracie had said yes to Connor's best friend, Dante Santangelo, of all people. It was a match that Ian never would have predicted. Gracie was a ray of sunshine. The way Ian remembered it, even as a kid, Dante had been a brooding, grim, too-serious sort of guy. Not so much anymore, though. Every time Dante looked at Gracie, he lit up from the inside.

Somehow, Ian got through all the introductions, the endless hugs and exclamations of wonder and excitement that he'd "come home" at last.

He didn't feel at home, not in the least. He felt awkward and uncomfortable and tried hard not to show it. They were good people, this family he'd forgotten for twenty years. He didn't want to hurt or insult them with the uncomfortable truth that, while he did recognize them, did know a lot about each of them as children, he didn't feel any true connection with a single one of them.

He felt like a phantom limb. Not really *there*, yet the family he'd been born into still considered him an actual, physical part of the family experience they shared.

Only the old people, the brother and sister octogenarians, Percy and Daffodil Valentine, seemed to have any clue of how he really felt. Percy spoke to him of the years they'd spent trying to find him, the dead ends they'd pursued, the promising leads that had come to nothing. Daffy treated him with care, gently patting his arm with her wrinkled, spotted hand, encouraging him to "take good care" of himself, to "give himself time to adjust"—whatever that meant.

Even the children seemed glad to see him.

Two-and-a-half-year-old Marie, Daniel and Keely's daughter, toddled right up to him and held up her arms. "Finn. Hug."

He resisted the urge to inform her that his name was not Finn and hadn't been for twenty years. Instead, he bent, scooped her up and submitted to her wrapping her chubby arms around his neck and planting a slobbery kiss on his cheek, after which she announced, "Wuv you." For that he'd managed a smile, to which she responded, "Down, now."

He set her on the floor next to the family basset hound, Maisey Fae, and she tottered off, the dog right behind her.

For him, the evening dragged on forever. Without Ella's help, he never would have made it through. If not for her, he would have run down the sloping front walk, jumped in the Lexus and burned rubber getting the hell out of there.

Ella didn't hover, but she stayed in sight. He only had to glance over and make eye contact with her. A minute later, she would appear at his side. He would feel for her hand. She would give it, slipping her fingers in his, gazing up at him with an easy smile. Her hand in his grounded him. Her touch said she understood, she had his back, she wouldn't vanish when he needed her.

Her smile somehow promised that everything would turn out right.

A couple of hours crawled by. He got through the meal and a brief one-on-one with each of his siblings save Aislinn—and Madison, the movie star, the blood sister he'd never met until tonight, the one who'd been switched with the Aislinn he remembered as his sister from all those years ago.

The few moments with Matthias had been the hardest. Matt had a wife now, Sabra, whom he clearly adored, and a newborn son, Adam, named after Sabra's deceased dad. Matt seemed tense. Ian sympathized. He felt the same, not about Matt specifically, but about all of it. About being here in Oregon, about dealing with all these people he'd finally remembered but didn't feel much actual connection to.

Ian sensed that Matt blamed himself for what had happened that long-ago day when the boy, Finn, had wandered away from the rest of the family. But in their brief conversation, Matt never broached the subject and Ian didn't really want to get into it, anyway. He did have the urge, though, to reassure Matt, to explain that by the time he'd spotted the small, white creature off the path in the snow, his grouchy older brother had been the last thing on his mind.

The right moment to say all that never exactly presented itself, so Ian just let it go.

And by then, he'd started seeing the light at

the end of the tunnel in terms of this excruciating evening. He began planning his escape. He just needed to say a quick thank-you to Daniel and Keely, grab Ella, and get out of there.

About then, Aislinn and Madison appeared on either side of him.

Madison—who should have been Aislinn—took his hand. Talk about bizarre. Hadn't she just won an Oscar a month or two ago? How many movies had he seen her in? Several. Never would he have guessed that America's darling would turn out to be his sister.

She had that Bravo look, though, golden hair and the blue eyes to go with it—also, a belly out to here. She and her husband, Sten Larson, expected their first child any day now.

"Come outside to the porch with us," said Madison.

"Just for a few minutes," added Aislinn, a petite woman with dark eyes and hair. Ironically enough, Aislinn looked like a movie star, too. Maybe Audrey Hepburn, or one of those French actresses with their pretty, big-eyed, delicate faces.

The two women guided him through the entry hall and out the front door. They were on the porch before he thought to object or shoot Ella one of his frantic, get-over-here-and-save-my-sorry-ass looks.

"Let's sit down, shall we?" said Aislinn. It wasn't really a question. They took him to a row of cushioned wicker chairs near one end of the long, deep porch and pulled him down into the center one. The two of them settled in the chairs to either side of his, flanking him, same as before.

"So how are you holding up?" asked Aislinn.

"Holding up? Good. Fine."

Those enormous dark eyes called him a liar. Her words were gentle, though. "You're in better shape than I was, then."

"Excuse me?"

"When I found out I wasn't really me, after all."

"Well, of course you're you," he argued, annoyed that she would say such a thing.

"Yeah, but I didn't feel like me when I found out that the woman I knew as my mother hadn't given birth to me, that I was no blood relation to my dad, whom I adored. That another woman had carried me inside her body and my birth father had switched me the night I was born, changed my life completely, in order not to have to acknowledge me. At first, it made me feel I was less than before. But over time, I've come to see that I really am still a Bravo—and I'm also the child of a secret affair between a woman I was never destined to meet and a man I had never liked in the least."

Madison chuckled, a rich and husky sound.

America's darling was famous for her laugh. "I was mostly just in denial after I found out. And when I did finally reach out to the family, I didn't even call first."

Now he felt defensive. "You mean, same as I did, showing up unannounced at Valentine Logging today, is that what you're getting at?"

"Finn," said Aislinn in a soothing tone. "It's not a criticism. We're only trying to say that we understand a little of what you must be going through."

"My name is Ian." He said it too fast—and much too harshly.

"Yes, of course, Ian," said Aislinn, her voice so calm, full of understanding. "I'm sorry."

Now he kind of hated himself. Aislinn only wanted to make him feel better, and he'd jumped all over her. "No, *I'm* sorry. I shouldn't get on you. That's how you knew me, as Finn."

Madison laughed again—a pained sound this time. "Believe it or not, we dragged you out here to reassure you that we understand a little of what you're going through. We know it's not easy, finding out that who you thought you were isn't the whole story—and no, your situation is not the same as ours, but there are certain similarities. We get how hard it is, we really do."

Aislinn added wryly, "Too bad we're just making it worse."

Complete the survey below and return it today to receive up to 4 FREE BOOKS and FREE GIFTS guaranteed!

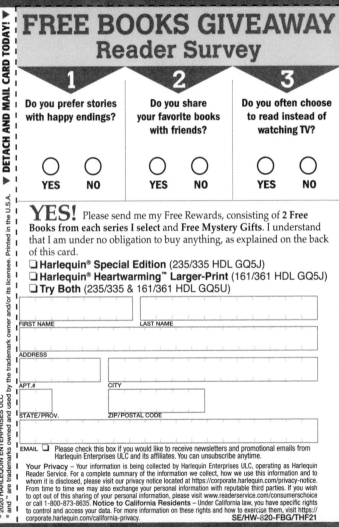

▼ DETACH AND MAIL CARD TODAY! ▼

FREE BOOKS GIVEAWAY
Reader Survey

1

Do you prefer stories with happy endings?

○ YES ○ NO

2

Do you share your favorite books with friends?

○ YES ○ NO

3

Do you often choose to read instead of watching TV?

○ YES ○ NO

YES! Please send me my Free Rewards, consisting of **2 Free Books from each series I select** and **Free Mystery Gifts**. I understand that I am under no obligation to buy anything, as explained on the back of this card.

❏ Harlequin® Special Edition (235/335 HDL GQ5J)
❏ Harlequin® Heartwarming™ Larger-Print (161/361 HDL GQ5J)
❏ Try Both (235/335 & 161/361 HDL GQ5U)

FIRST NAME

LAST NAME

ADDRESS

APT.#

CITY

STATE/PROV.

ZIP/POSTAL CODE

EMAIL ❏ Please check this box if you would like to receive newsletters and promotional emails from Harlequin Enterprises ULC and its affiliates. You can unsubscribe anytime.

BUSINESS REPLY MAIL
FIRST-CLASS MAIL   PERMIT NO. 717   BUFFALO, NY

POSTAGE WILL BE PAID BY ADDRESSEE

HARLEQUIN READER SERVICE
PO BOX 1341
BUFFALO NY 14240-8571

NO POSTAGE
NECESSARY
IF MAILED
IN THE
UNITED STATES

Before he could figure out what to say next, the front door opened, and Ella stepped out.

Had he ever been so relieved to see anyone? Doubtful. He jumped up and went to her as Matthias came out behind her.

Ella gazed up at him, a frown between her brows. "Are we interrupting?"

"Of course not," said Aislinn.

Madison added, "We were just trying to be helpful—too bad we failed miserably."

Even Ian chuckled at that. "Not true." It was a flat-out lie. He didn't feel the least helped by what had just transpired, but Madison and Aislinn had the best of intentions. He refused to give them any more grief for making an effort with him. "And really, we should get going." No, they shouldn't. They should stick around, spend more time with this family he'd just found. But he couldn't. He only wanted out of there—and the sooner the better, as far as he was concerned. "I'll just run in and thank Daniel and Keely."

"No need," said Madison.

"You sure?" He should go in and say goodbye properly. But then somebody else would probably try to get him talking...

"Go," said Aislinn. "It's obvious you've had enough Bravo family togetherness for one night.

We'll thank Daniel for you. It's not a problem, I promise you."

"All right, then." He took Ella's hand and felt instantly better.

But then Matt said, "One more thing…"

Irrational dread crawling up the back of his neck, Ian turned to the last familiar face he'd seen before he veered off that snowy path twenty years ago and his life changed forever. "Sure." Somehow, he managed to make the word sound friendly.

"Daniel says you're here through Sunday?"

"Leaving early Monday morning, yes."

"So we were thinking tomorrow we could make it a day, just the Bravo brothers—you, me, Daniel, Connor and Liam. Liam's got a new boat. We'll take it out, the five of us."

Stuck on a boat with four virtual strangers who happened to be his brothers. He didn't want to go.

But Ella squeezed his hand. "Sounds great." She turned those big eyes on him. Those eyes said, *You need to do it. This is what you're here for.*

Did she have to be so damn right? "Thanks, I would like that," he said, not liking it in the least.

Matt looked relieved. "Wonderful. We'll text you the time and place to meet."

"I've got an idea." Aislinn grinned at Madison. "While the Bravo brothers are out on the boat, the rest of us ought to get together, whoever can make it. We'll grill some steaks out at Wild River." Aislinn lived with her husband, Jax, up near Astoria at his ranch, Wild River.

Madison rubbed her giant stomach. "Absolutely—Ella, you in?"

"Yes." Ella sent the sisters her glowing smile. "I'm so there." She looked honestly pleased at the invitation. In fact, she'd seemed to enjoy the whole evening. She should bottle that enthusiasm and share it with him.

"Good." Madison nodded her approval. "I'm guessing Karin will want to come." Karin was Liam's wife—and Sten's sister. The Bravos were a study in complex family relationships. Ian could barely keep them all straight. "We'll make the calls, get it all worked out. And we'll pick you up, Ella."

Ella beamed. "Wonderful. Connor has my number. Text me everything I need to know."

As Ian pulled her down the steps and along the walk to the car, she gave the three on the porch one last wave. He walked faster. The quicker they got away, the less likely some random Bravo would find a reason to call them back.

Ian said nothing on the return trip to the inn. Ella didn't mind. He seemed pretty stressed, and usually, when Ian felt stressed, it worked out better simply to leave the man alone.

If he needed to talk about it, he would. If not, she had a feeling there would be lots of manly sharing tomorrow on Liam's new boat. Ian would get more than he'd ever wanted of meaningful conversation then. For now, a little peace and quiet seemed the best way to go.

They entered their suite at a few minutes after nine. Would he want to be alone tonight?

Most likely.

That made her sad. Now that she'd thrown caution and good sense to the wind and slept with him, she didn't want to miss her chance to do it again. At breakfast, he'd asked her to consider sharing more nights—three nights, to be specific, until they returned to New York.

She wanted those nights.

But what she wanted didn't come first, not now. This trip wasn't about her. After an evening with all the relatives he hadn't seen in twenty years, he probably needed to be left alone to rest and recuperate. The exhaustion in his eyes said he required time to recover from all the family togetherness.

As he shut the door to the outer hallway and she flicked on one of the sitting room lamps, their phones buzzed, one right after the other. He pulled his from his pocket as she did the same.

He held his phone up, screen out. "All the information I ever needed about hanging with my brothers tomorrow on Liam's boat."

"And mine's from Aislinn. They'll be here to pick me up at eleven. I should wear something I can ride a horse in, and if I don't have boots, Aislinn thinks she has some that will work for me." She widened her eyes. "Horseback riding is not my best event. I'm going to need the slow, sweet, *old* horse."

"I'm sure Aislinn can arrange for that." He put his phone away.

They regarded each other across the distance from the sofa to the door. She thought about last night and this afternoon, about kissing him, about all the lovely things he'd done to her body.

And then she put those thoughts away. "All right, then. I think I'll take a long bath and try to get a good night's sleep." She turned for the open door to her room.

He moved silently. One moment he stood by the door and the next, he was right behind her. "Hey."

Excitement quivered through her. "Hmm?"

He stepped in even closer. Havoc erupted within her as he eased her hair away from her neck, his warm finger brushing her nape, sending sparks of sensation flaring across her skin. "Are you having second thoughts, Ell?" His voice was soft yet rough, a whisper of sandpaper in her ear.

"Um, not exactly." Her own voice sounded strange to her—young and hesitant and so very serious.

"But you're going to your room alone anyway?"

With a careful sigh, she let herself lean back against him. He felt so warm. So solid and strong. "After all the togetherness at Daniel's house, I thought maybe you would need a little time to yourself."

Now he put both hands on her, one on each shoulder. His thumbs traced a burning path on either side of her throat—down and then up and then down again. "What I need is another night with you."

A lovely shiver went through her. "More than you need time alone?"

He laughed then, a low sound, both rough and tender. "Hell, yes."

Anticipation filling her belly with butterflies, she turned to look up into his waiting eyes. "Well, then yes, please. I would love another night with you."

He stared down at her for the longest time.

"What?" she demanded.

"For a moment there, I just knew that you would

pull away, go through that door and shut it behind you."

She laughed. Because he wanted her and she wanted him and no matter what, tonight would be fabulous. Okay, fine. Just maybe she'd made the big mistake of falling in love with him. So what? People gave their hearts all the time. Sometimes it didn't work out. Once they returned home, she would just have to learn to get over him, to move on. "It did occur to me that maybe we shouldn't…"

He cut her off with a finger to her lips. "Not. Another. Word—except yes. I'll take a yes."

She went on tiptoe and whispered in his ear. "Yes."

"Right answer." He bent just long enough to scoop her high in his arms.

Ella woke very late, naked in Ian's bed.

He'd thrown an arm across her upper chest, and one big leg rested on her thighs.

Yes, it had been touch-and-go at Daniel's. But boy, did things get good later. She might possibly have beard burn on her face and inner thighs. Also, muscles she'd forgotten she had ached in the loveliest sort of way.

Beard burn and muscle aches had never felt so good.

Now came the big question. Should she ease

out from under the warm weight of his hold and go back to her own room?

She felt a little unsure about the idea of facing daylight in his bed—or more specifically, waking up in daylight beside him. Why that seemed a bridge too far, she couldn't really say.

However, yesterday morning, when she'd emerged from her room to find him on his laptop in the sitting area, he'd said nothing about the way she'd left his bed during the night. Could she assume that he approved of her leaving before morning?

It seemed very *Ian* to want a woman in his bed but then to prefer not to wake up beside her— and really, that was just sad. She frowned into the darkness.

Get over yourself, Haralson. You knew who he was when you climbed in his bed.

Yes, she'd have a price to pay for this stolen fling with her boss and good friend.

And what about the whole love question?

At some point, she'd have to face that head-on, too.

But she'd made a conscious decision to enjoy this time with him. She needed to stop second-guessing every little thing, needed to give herself completely to loving every minute of the few nights they would have together.

"Don't even think about it." His sleep-rough voice interrupted her silent debate with herself.

She hardly had to move at all to press her forehead to his. "I didn't know you were awake."

"You woke me up," he whisper-grumbled.

"How? I didn't say a word or move a muscle."

"Yeah, but you're thinking of going back to your room, aren't you?"

She almost giggled, which was nothing short of ridiculous. She'd never been the giggly type. Until now, apparently. "Okay, yeah. Let's call it an internal dialogue, a silent discussion of the pros and cons of leaving versus staying here with you."

"The way I understand it, you need two people to have a dialogue."

"Of course you would believe that. You're a man."

His arm tightened across her chest as he pressed his lower leg against the outside of her knee, pulling her closer. "There are no pros to leaving my room."

"Sure there are."

"Name them."

"In my room, I get the bed all to myself."

"That's one—and not a particularly good one. Stay."

"Hmm." She kissed the space between his eyebrows. "I admit, I'm tempted."

He nuzzled closer, catching her chin between his teeth, biting down gently and then laying a light trail of kisses up over her cheek to her ear, where he whispered, "I think I need to up my game."

"Nobody's stopping you."

He kissed her. And then he rolled her under him and kissed her some more.

After the third kiss, he lifted his head and met her gaze through the shadows. "So then. Staying or going?"

"I have no idea what you're talking about. Kiss me again…"

In the morning, Ian woke to find Ella in the bed beside him.

What a great moment—opening his eyes and finding her there, her hair all over the place, her lips slightly parted as she snored softly.

Cutest thing he'd ever seen. Made him hard, too.

So he reached out, pulled her close and showed her how happy he was to see her. Sex with his best friend had turned out to be something of a revelation. Who knew his good buddy Ella would be amazing in bed?

Certainly not him. How could he have known? Up till Thursday night, he'd never let himself think of her that way.

But as of now, well, he couldn't help thinking

that barging in on Ella in her sexy bra and tiny thong had been a great move, after all. Talk about seeing a woman in a whole new light—and then he'd gotten lucky. She'd said yes to him. Now he could touch her and hold her and make her moan his name.

The disorientation and confusion he experienced whenever he had to deal with his newfound family aside, this trip to the Pacific Northwest had turned out to be one hell of a wonderful time—the best time he'd had in a long while. He intended to love every minute of this thing with her. It would end much too soon.

Tonight and tomorrow just plain weren't long enough.

Already, he found himself imagining ways to convince her they should continue together like this after they got home.

But he wouldn't. They would cut it clean then, as they'd agreed.

And no, he couldn't predict how things would go between them when it was over. They might have a rough patch as they dealt with going back to friends and colleagues only.

But one way or another, he knew they would make it work. He had faith in him and Ella, as a team.

Chapter Eight

After breakfast, back in the suite, Ian wanted to drag Ella straight to his bed. They had a little time before he had to meet his brothers.

But they had Abby to consider.

They video chatted with her on his laptop. The kid wanted to know all about the Bravos. She said she couldn't wait to meet them. She wished she'd made the trip with them, that she could go on the boat with Ian and his brothers—and she wanted to spend a day on horseback at Wild River Ranch, too.

He felt uncomfortable listening to her go on about tagging along the next time he flew out to

Oregon. Because thinking about returning? Right now, he couldn't say for certain that he would get through *this* visit without losing his shit.

No way he wanted to imagine coming back.

Why would he?

He'd severed his connection to the Bravos and this town, severed it by necessity when Siberia swallowed him whole. Somewhere between the bear attack, the grim horror of the hospital and the misery of the orphanage, he'd let the Bravos go in order to survive.

He got it now—the pain of losing his family, of his complete aloneness in a strange land where no one spoke words he could understand, had been unbearable. So he'd recreated himself as the scarred, mute boy with no history and no family— a boy who felt nothing, who only survived.

And then Glynis had come. He'd known hope for the first time he could remember. And when she took him home with her, he'd recreated himself a second time, as her son.

So what if a few old memories of his life as Finn Bravo had finally come back to him? Reclaimed memories didn't suddenly make him a grown-up version of his childhood self. He'd come here to face the past, yeah. He hated it, but he felt driven to do it, anyway. And then he would be done with it.

On Monday, he and Ella would go home.

End of story. Back to real life.

Abby wheedled, "I'm thinking we should visit at Christmastime, you know? We could all three—you, me and Mom—go to Oregon together. Not for Christmas Day or anything, but sometime during my Christmas vacation. Like as soon as I get off school. That would work great. I've never seen the Pacific Ocean. It's about time I did."

"It's doubtful that will happen," he said carefully, reluctant as always to say no to her outright.

"But *maybe*?" Abby twinkled at him, showing off the cute dimples in her round cheeks. "Just think about it, Ian. It could be so much fun."

Ella came to his rescue with a single word. "Abigail." She said it gently, but Abby always got the message when her mother used her full name.

The dimples faded, but Abby's smile never wavered. "Okay, then. We can talk about it some other time, I guess…"

When they wrapped it up a few minutes later, it was time for him to go meet the Bravo brothers.

He hesitated at the door. Madison wouldn't arrive to pick up Ella for another hour or so. "I hate to leave you here alone."

"Why?" Ella, looking very country in snug jeans and a plaid button-up, had followed him to the little square of entry hallway. "Even if for some reason the visit to Wild River gets canceled, I'm hardly going to suffer while hanging at the beach in our luxury suite. And they do have a spa here, you know? I could get myself a hot rock massage and a fresh mani-pedi."

He couldn't keep his hands off her. Reaching out, he eased his fingers under the satiny fall of her hair and wrapped them around the nape of her neck. "Now I'm jealous."

"Of what?"

"Whoever gets to put their hands on you, gets to give you a massage and paint your toenails. I'm surprisingly good at massage, and I wouldn't mind polishing those pretty toes for you. Maybe we should both just stay here." He pulled her closer, until she was right up against him, so slim and soft and flexible, but wearing way too many clothes. With his free hand, he toyed with the top button on her shirt.

She wrapped her fingers around his and gently pushed them away. "You didn't come all the way across the country to hang out in the room and paint my toenails for me."

He made use of the hand still curled around her nape to ease her in nice and close to him again. Conveniently, she tipped her head back a little, bringing her sweet mouth within a couple of inches of his.

"All right then," he bargained, "forget the massage and pedicure. Concentrate on you and me and the two big beds in this suite. We haven't tried out your bed yet. We need to do that—and come to think of it, who needs a bed? We could make use of the sofa or maybe that club chair over there."

"I think you've become obsessed with sex."

"I have, yes. I need it. But within specific parameters."

"Wow. You've got parameters now?"

"Yeah. I need a lot of sex, and it needs to be with you." He dipped his head enough to brush his lips across hers. "You complaining?"

"I most definitely am not."

He took a longer kiss the second time.

She let out a soft sigh, and he really did consider blowing off the Bravos and doing something a lot more fun.

But then she gave him a gentle shove. "You've got somewhere you need to be. Go meet your brothers."

Five minutes later, he was behind the wheel, heading north on 101.

Liam Bravo had texted Ian directions to West Basin Marina in the Port of Astoria, where Liam docked his boat.

Ian parked his car in the marina lot and found Connor waiting for him at the end of the specified dock. As they climbed aboard the thirty-four-foot cruiser, Ian saw that he was the last to arrive. Great-Uncle Percy had come, too.

Once out on the water, they passed under the Astoria-Megler Bridge that connected Oregon to Washington State. Drinking local craft beer, with Liam at the helm, they soared up the wide Columbia. Ian enjoyed the spectacular views and felt grateful that none of his brothers or the ancient great-uncle tried to get him talking about anything too uncomfortable—like life in a Russian orphanage or how it had been for him not remembering his family of origin for most of his life so far. Percy had brought the DNA kits. He took cheek swabs from Daniel and Ian—swabbing more Bravos wasn't necessary. The whole family had been tested when they found out that Aislinn and Madison were switched at birth.

The results of this test, Percy promised, would come through by the middle of next week.

The middle of next week...

By then, Ian and Ella would be home in New York. Not that it really mattered to the Bravos. They all considered the test nothing more than a formality. They just *knew*, they all said, that he was the brother they'd lost so long ago.

He envied them their trust, the way they so effortlessly accepted him as one of theirs. And he wished he could be more like them—yeah, he knew them, recognized them as the people in his newly recovered memories. But they had no such proof that he told the truth. He could be scamming them, looking for some kind of payoff, for all they knew.

That made him grateful for the ease of DNA testing. By Tuesday, if any of them harbored secret doubts about the truth of his claim, they could let them go.

And he could move on. He had no expectations to get close to them, and he hoped none of them decided they ought to visit him in Manhattan.

In the early afternoon, they docked at a small marina on the Washington side of the river near a pretty little country town. A five-minute walk from the boat slip took them to a tree-shaded, parklike area at the river's edge.

Ian helped haul the folding chairs Liam kept stowed on the boat. Connor and Matthias had taken charge of the food. They'd packed four big picnic baskets full of sausages and cheeses, smoked salmon, crackers and artisan breads. Also on offer, more local beer and some Oregon pinot noir.

Everyone helped to lay it all out on a picnic table and they sat around sipping their drinks, enjoying the food. The talk remained casual—for a while.

Then old Uncle Percy asked about Glynis. Ian told them the story of how she came to the orphanage for a baby and ended up taking home the mute boy with all the ugly scars.

He explained how she'd died trying to screw in a lightbulb. "She was always so independent. Whatever little job needed doing, her first response was, 'I can do that myself.'"

"You miss her very much," said Percy.

"Every day. Her father died when she was ten and she spent the rest of her growing-up years in the system, but she never seemed damaged by that. She had boyfriends. Lots of them, right up until the end, though she never got married or had kids—except me. Nothing could dampen her enthusiasm for life. She was always upbeat, ready to take on the world."

His description of Glynis seemed to open the floodgates. Every brother had a question. Ian got it. Even if he felt a certain distance from them, they considered him *theirs*, somehow. He ended up telling them a sanitized version of life in the orphanage and what he remembered of his encounter with the bear.

Liam passed him another beer. "Still no clue how you ended up so far from Irkutsk?"

He screwed off the top. Since he'd talked to Ella about this a week ago, more memories had come to him, mostly at night during weird, disjointed dreams. "I have a vague memory that someone picked me up on a road after I wandered away from the family. I'm fairly sure that was before the bear attacked me. I flagged a truck down, I think. No way I could have flagged a ride after the bear got through with me. It's not clear to me, not any of what happened before I woke up in the hospital. All I've got are random flashes—a ride in a rattletrap truck, hiding in a barn somewhere, setting out on foot again, hungry but too scared to approach anyone. I remember deep woods, this strange silence—and the bear coming at me out of nowhere…"

And he'd said way too much. Shaking his head, he took a long pull off that fresh beer.

The men raised their drinks high.

"To you, Ian," said Daniel.

A murmur of agreement went up.

After that, he made a point to ask questions—about who went to college where, how they met their wives. He got them talking about their children, all of whom had been at Daniel's the night before. People loved to talk about their kids. Most of the brothers' children were babies. But Liam, who had a twenty-month-old son with his wife, Karin, also had two stepkids, a boy and a girl. Ian encouraged him to go on about the brilliant stepson's latest science project. The stepdaughter, Coco, sounded a lot like Abby. All the brothers agreed that Coco could outtalk a politician on Election Day and charm the most hardened of hearts.

Mostly, for the rest of the afternoon, during the boat ride farther upriver before Liam finally turned them around and headed back the way they'd come, Ian took care not to let too much lag occur in the conversation. He steered the talk to subjects other than himself and he did it skillfully, from years of practice. Talking about himself made him feel weak, unprotected.

Better not to go there.

In the meantime, at Wild River Ranch on the Youngs River ten miles south of Astoria, Ella had a great time with the Bravo sisters. She met Aislinn's huge, fluffy German angora rabbits, Bunbun and Luna, who lived on the enclosed porch of the ranch house. Bunbun came right to her, fluffy ears twitching. Aislinn had carrot tops to tempt him. He ate them straight from Ella's hand.

As promised, Aislinn produced a pair of sturdy rawhide boots for Ella to wear. Burt, the ranch foreman, gave her the gentlest gelding in the stable for a horseback tour of the ranch. Burt's border collie, Ace, joined them. The dog happily ran alongside them, circling back to take up the rear whenever one of the sisters activated his herding instincts by lagging too far behind the others.

They got back to the ranch house in the late afternoon. The Bravo sisters' husbands had fired up the grill. In the shade of a couple of giant bigleaf maple trees, they ate thick steaks and marinated chicken and so many sides Ella couldn't possibly do justice to them all. She settled on potato salad, corn on the cob, and artichoke and tomato panzanella. It was all delicious. She ate more than she should have and would have gone back for more if she hadn't been so full.

The early-May weather was lovely—sunny, but not too hot, with a light breeze. The men cleared off the meal and left Ella and Ian's sisters under the trees with pitchers of excellent margaritas to share.

"Who has all the kids today?" Ella asked. "I'm guessing they're not on the boat with the guys."

"You guessed right," said Madison. "Keely, Sabra, Aly and Karin—" she rattled off the names of the Bravo brothers' wives "—took all the cousins to the beach. Grandpa Otto and Aunt Daffy are pitching in there, too." Ella felt reasonably certain that Grandpa Otto was Karin and Sten's father. With so much family around, she found it quite the challenge to keep all the relationships straight.

"That way, we get to have you all to ourselves and the guys get Ian." Patting her enormous belly,

Madison raised her glass of iced strawberry-leaf tea in a toast before taking a sip.

Ella eyed her sideways. "To do what, exactly?"

"To get to know you, of course," Hailey, born seventh of the siblings, replied with a big grin. "Us girls get to pump you for juicy information and the guys get a little quality time with their long-lost brother."

Ella could picture it all too clearly—Ian, alone on a boat with the brothers he'd just met. She hoped he was getting through the experience without too much anxiety. "Ian's a private sort of man."

More than one Bravo sister chuckled. Aislinn said, "We noticed that."

Ella continued, "I've worked with him for almost a decade. He considers me his best friend, but sometimes I wonder if *I* even know him." As the words came out of her mouth, she suspected she'd said too much. She should go easy on the margaritas. But Aislinn stood beside her with the pitcher, and she automatically offered her glass for a refill.

"We're just glad you showed up on a weekend." Harper, born ten months after Hailey, had the trademark wheat-blond hair and blue eyes of all the sisters, save Aislinn. "Weekdays can be crazy, with the kids and the jobs." Harper and her husband, Linc, lived in Portland with his little niece and nephew. Linc had taken custody of the two children when his sister and her husband died in a plane crash over a year before. "It's nice to have more than one day with you guys, nice to get time with you alone, Ella, to get to know all the good stuff, about you and Ian and the two of you together."

Warmth curled through Ella, that the Bravo sisters wanted to get to know her better—but then she wondered why, exactly? She was no long-lost sibling.

She sat up straighter in her lounge chair. "Wait a minute." Sweeping out a hand around the circle of women, she accused, "You all think that Ian and I are a couple, don't you? Like dating. You think we're dating?"

Gracie scoffed. "Dating? I don't know if that's the word I would've used."

"Yeah," agreed Hailey. "You two are way past dating."

"*Together.*" Aislinn gave a firm nod. "That's a good word. You two are clearly together."

"Wait, what?" It felt all wrong to let them assume such a thing. Ian wouldn't like it, and she... Well, she needed to keep her head on straight vis-à-vis the situation with Ian. "No, Ian and I are not *together*, not in the way that you mean. We're *friends*. And we work together—we do that very well together, as a matter of fact. We have an excellent working relationship. We are best friends who work together. That's the only kind of *together* we are."

Except for the great sex we're currently having, she couldn't help mentally confessing. Because, fine. Okay, there was that. But only until they returned to New York.

And why did the thought that the great sex would come to an abrupt forever end on Monday morning make her feel so ridiculously sad?

"You look so sad all of a sudden." Gracie leaned close and briefly clasped Ella's arm, after which she asked softly, "How long have you been in love with him?"

Ella stifled a gasp as she flashed back to that day at Manhattan General, to Lucinda in her red-soled shoes, tossing her long blond curls, accusing... *Everyone knows you're in love with him. It's pathetic.*

Apparently, Lucinda was right. *And Marisol*, Ella grudgingly added. *Let us not forget Marisol.* And now, even here in Oregon, all the way on the other side of the continent, Ian's long-lost baby sister knew. And just by looking at her, apparently. Just by seeing her with Ian.

Ella drank the rest of her margarita in one long swallow. "Not touching that one."

Gracie wouldn't stop. "Are you saying he doesn't know how you feel?" she asked, incredulous, as Ella envisioned herself jumping up and running off screaming. Did everyone think she carried a torch for Ian?

Aislinn said, "Gracie." When Gracie glanced over, Aislinn shook her head.

Gracie groaned. "What's wrong with my saying it? It's not like it's a bad thing. And it's so totally obvious that he's in love with her, too."

Ian *loved* her? For a moment, Ella's heart felt light as a moonbeam.

But no. Ian didn't do love. Ella had always known that—and if she hadn't known, he'd said it right to her face in the darkest hours of Friday morning, before they'd made love for the first time. Gracie had only misread Ian's signals. She thought she saw romantic love, but she was wrong. She saw the respect and affection Ella and Ian had for each other—that, and maybe a hint of the sexual tension currently zapping back and forth between them. Gracie saw all that and assumed it meant more than it did.

"Aw, Ella," Gracie said gently.

Ella hardly had time to set down her drink before the youngest Bravo sister leaped from her chair, grabbed Ella's hand and pulled her up into a hug.

"You'll work it out," Gracie whispered in her ear.

Ella enjoyed the hug and whispered back, "I hope so. I really do."

Ian got through the remainder of the afternoon with his brothers well enough, he thought. After those few touch-and-go moments when he'd said more than he should have about what had gone down twenty years ago in Russia, he'd managed to keep the conversation from straying in that direction again.

Both Daniel and Connor brought up future visits—that they would come to him in New York and that he would return to Valentine Bay to spend time with the family. He kept his replies to that line of questioning vague, managing not to make any commitments either way.

But he probably should have known he wouldn't get away clean. As they docked in Astoria, Liam brought up Hailey's wedding. She and her fiancé, Roman Marek, would be married on the last Saturday of the month.

"Check your calendar," said Daniel. "We would all love it if you could make it for that…"

Ian played along. What else could he do? He clapped his oldest brother on the shoulder and said he'd get back to them about it.

Uncle Percy promised that the DNA results

would go out to everyone by Wednesday at the latest. Liam thanked the old guy and said goodbye to his brothers.

It was almost six when he finally climbed in the Lexus and headed back to the Isabel Inn, where he found Ella sitting on the sofa, channel surfing, still wearing the jeans and plaid shirt she'd put on that morning for her day at the ranch.

So cute. She'd drawn her bare feet up onto the cushions and caught her tongue between her teeth as she concentrated on the screen.

Just the sight of her made everything better. The knots of tension at the back of his neck and in his shoulders from a day of avoiding too much focus on the past melted away.

She'd piled all that gorgeous hair up into a topknot. He wanted to grab her and drag her straight to his room, where he would peel off that shirt, take down those jeans and undo her topknot. He couldn't wait to get up close and personal with those long, sexy legs and small, sensitive breasts.

He tossed his Yankees cap on the table. "When did you get back?"

"Madison dropped me off about fifteen minutes ago." She turned off the big screen and set the remote on the stack of coffee table books. "You want to go eat?"

"I'll go with you if you're hungry, but we pretty much ate all day long. And there was beer. Lots of beer."

She laughed. "I hear you. Let's skip dinner, then. You should have seen the pile of steak and chicken I put away—no beer, though. But there might have been one too many margaritas."

"Did you ride a horse?"

"Damn straight."

"Ella, the cowgirl." He sat down beside her and shucked off his Docksiders. "I wish I'd seen that."

"Missed your chance. It's so sad…" She made a frowny face—and those delicate lips of hers? They cried out for his kiss.

"C'mere." He hooked an arm across her shoulders and pulled her against him, taking her mouth and wrapping her up good and tight in his hold. She tasted so good—both sweet and tart. And she smelled like coconut and a field of clover.

When she pulled away, he reached over and tugged on that topknot.

"Hey!" She slapped at him playfully as her hair came undone, the dark waves cascading down over her shoulders.

"Beautiful," he said, and stuck his nose in it, breathing in deep.

She whacked him again, this time with the back

of her hand. "You're kind of a hair pervert, you know that?"

He scoffed. "There's no such thing as a hair pervert."

"Yes, there is. Look it up. It's a person who is overly obsessed with someone's hair. I think they used your picture as part of the definition."

He sniffed her hair. Because it smelled so good. "You're sure about that?"

"Beyond the faintest shadow of a doubt."

"All right, then." He might just as well own it. "Yes, I am obsessed with your hair and damn proud of it, too." He levered backward, pulling her down on top of him as he stretched out across the cushions.

She braced her hands on either side of him and craned back to fake a glare at him. "Let me go. I need a shower."

"No, you don't." Her unbound hair brushed his chest and tickled his neck. He got a hank of it and brought it to his face. "You smell amazing."

"No doubt about it. You're a bad man, a hair pervert."

He eased his fingers up under all that wonderful hair and cradled the back of her head so he could bring her mouth to his again. When only a whisper of space separated them, he suggested, "Let me show you just how bad I am…"

* * *

By the time they moved from the sofa to his bed, Ian felt good about everything. Life was amazing and he wanted Ella in his arms all night and all day tomorrow. He needed not to waste a moment. They had an agreement and the agreement had a deadline. He intended to honor it.

Already, he hated Monday. It would come much too soon.

He decided not to think about that, to focus on right now—which was spectacular.

He pulled her down to the mattress and made love to her a second time. Slowly. Savoring every sigh he wrung from her, every moan, every sharp, indrawn breath.

At a little before nine, they both needed fuel. He called room service and ordered one of their fancy pizzas. When it came, he pulled on a pair of sweats and answered the door.

Back in the bedroom, he found her sitting cross-legged on the bed wearing his shirt.

"Sparkling water?" he asked. At her nod, he handed her the pizza and returned to the main room to get the waters from the snack fridge.

"You look good in my shirt," he said as he joined her on the bed.

She grinned. "Royal blue. It's my color."

"Naked is still better."

"Treat me right. You might get lucky again tonight." Ella devoured her first slice in silence, but when she started on the second, she asked, "So how did it go today with your brothers?"

He knocked back a long swallow of sparkling water and considered what kind of answer to give her. With Ella, honesty seemed the wisest course. She tended to see right through him, anyway, when he tried to fake it. Just saying he didn't want to talk about it wouldn't work. If he didn't want to talk about it, that meant something had gone wrong and she would want to know what.

She might leave him alone about it for now. But eventually, she would circle back around to finding out whatever troubled him. She considered that her job as his friend.

Picking a slice of locally crafted pepperoni off her pizza, she popped it into her mouth. "That bad, huh?"

He shook himself. "No, not at all. They were great."

"But?"

One way or another, he would be sharing. Might as well get it over with. "Percy asked me what Glynis was like. I started telling him, and somehow I found myself babbling about my fragmented memories of how I ended up in a hospital in Krasnoyarsk."

"And there's something wrong with your talking to your brothers about what happened in Russia?"

"Not wrong, just…"

Just what? He had no idea what. He hardly knew where to go from here. But she looked at him so hopefully, eager to listen to his crap, to help him any way she could.

He made himself continue. "I mean, come on. It's clear that they're good people, the Bravos. And yes, I remember them now. I know that they're my family, biologically speaking. But I've had eighteen years of being Ian McNeill now. That's who I really am. Finn Bravo doesn't exist anymore."

She had that look, like she wanted to say something but wasn't sure she should.

"Just say it," he grumbled.

"I don't see why you have to deny the boy you were, that's all. You *are* Ian McNeill. But you started out as Finn Bravo. In that sense, Finn Bravo is part of you, too."

He wanted to grab her and shake her and somehow *make* her see. "He's not. He's gone—and as for my brothers and sisters, I never missed them, not in all this time. And now, it's like this is a big deal to them, but they're just strangers to me. I don't feel what they seem to feel, that sense of connection, or whatever."

They sat cross-legged on the bed, face-to-face.

She dropped her pizza crust on the tray between them and put her hand on his knee, a touch he knew she meant to ground him, reassure him.

Too bad it only made him feel more disconnected than ever. "I don't get it, what they feel. That's all. They act like they care so much about me, and they don't even know me."

She watched him so closely. That was the miracle of Ella. She had so much heart and she saw things other people didn't. He knew the exact moment she understood that he didn't want to be touched right now.

Slowly, she withdrew her hand. "I don't pretend to have answers for you—but I *can* say that I'm sure the reason your brothers seem to care is because they *do* care."

"Ell." He gave a laugh with no humor in it. "I agree. I think they *do* care. I just don't know how to deal with that—with love, you know? I don't 'get' love." Her sweet mouth twisted. He knew that look. He accused, "I can tell by your face that you don't believe me."

"Well, yeah. You're right. I don't. Because I know you. I know that you *do* feel love. You understand it. You give it. You loved Glynis and you still miss her so much."

"Glynis was different."

"Different than what?"

"Different than anyone else for me. She found me. She *saved* me. I became Ian McNeill because of her. I owe her everything."

"And you loved her. You still do. You honor her memory. You always will—and what about Abby? Are you actually going to try to tell me that you don't love Abby?"

"Of course I love Abby. What's not to love? She's smart and fun and bighearted. And she's already got a mom and a dad and a stepmom. Everybody jokes that I'm her other dad, but really, she's just a great kid—somebody else's kid. I'm not on the front lines for her the way you are, the way Philip is."

Ella's mouth had drawn down at the corners. "Ian, I don't even know what to say to you when you get like this."

He frowned back at her. At the same time, he thought how lucky he was to have a friend like her. He went ahead and said it. "And I love *you*, Ella."

He couldn't read her expression now. What did she feel? "I know you do," she said, then added softly, her tone just a little bit flat, "And I love you."

"We're friends," he said. "I care for you. But that's not the same as finding the one person for you, getting married and building a family together, the way all my newfound brothers and sisters seem to have done. I just don't get all that. I don't get the forever thing, that coupled-up thing, and I don't get the family thing. It's like a language I don't speak, one that's nothing but gibberish to me."

Ella stared at him. He had no idea what she might be thinking.

But he did have a scary feeling that he'd hurt her somehow, that she would jump from the bed and storm out the way all his ex-girlfriends had, that he'd pushed her too far. That she'd reached a hard limit with him and his inability to give what other normal, less screwed-up people not only gave, but needed themselves.

He was going to lose her friendship because he couldn't give her more than three days in Oregon. He knew it absolutely, then.

He would lose Ella—maybe not today. Maybe not next week.

But eventually, it would happen.

He would lose her, and when he did, he had no idea what he would do without her—and whoa!

Hold on just a minute.

No. Uh-uh. Not going to happen. Ella was far too reasonable and levelheaded to let this hot, temporary thing between them do permanent damage to what really mattered—their longtime friendship.

When the sexy times were over, they would still

have their friendship, still be a team at Patch&Pebble.
He could never lose her.

She wouldn't let that happen.

And he would not allow it.

Chapter Nine

This is not news, Ella sternly reminded herself. Ian had issues, and those issues wouldn't be resolved in this one painful heart-to-heart tonight.

She wished she didn't feel so miserable suddenly, but she couldn't help thinking that she'd only set herself up for misery when she'd said yes to this while-we're-in-Oregon fling.

She'd asked for trouble, and she would get it.

Could a guy make it any clearer that falling in love with him would bring a woman nothing but heartache? If she had any sense, she would end this thing with him now. Get up off this bed, go back to her own room and firmly shut the door.

Because, seriously, what had she thought would happen? Every touch of his hand, every thrilling brush of his lips to hers, brought her just that much closer to admitting what she'd tried for weeks now to deny.

Love. The word whispered through her mind, taunting her.

Yeah. She was a fool not to get out of here immediately.

However...

Except for this awful conversation that she herself had pushed him to engage in, this visit to Oregon had been nothing short of stellar.

While helping him deal with his newfound family, she'd had an amazing time with him, a fantasy weekend, a romantic, sexy getaway with a gorgeous man who knew his way around a woman's body.

And that brought her to the big question. Exactly how many fantasy weekends had she enjoyed in her life?

Answer: one. *This* one.

She'd spent a whole bunch of years looking for something she'd yet to find—love and forever with the right man, a family to call her own. Great sex just for fun had never been something she would allow herself to indulge in.

Even way back in high school, when she and Philip had made their fateful agreement, the purpose had been to learn about sex in the interest of being reasonably good at it when the right person came along. They'd married only to appease his parents and, when the time came, they'd gone through with their sworn promise to each other and gotten a divorce.

After the divorce, she'd always made sure she felt at least a hint of possibility that a guy might be her lifetime match before she would even go out with him. She'd had four sexual partners, total—Ian and Philip, and two other men. Both of those other men had wanted what she wanted: love and forever, with the right person. Neither of those relationships had gone all the way to a walk down the aisle.

And none of the others—including Philip—could come within miles of Ian sexually.

She had to be realistic. She'd reached the big three-oh without finding the one for her. She might never find that special man, the one who not only lit her up like a five-alarm fire but also couldn't wait to spend the rest of his life at her side.

At least now she knew how it felt to burn for the touch of a certain special someone—and to know that when he *did* touch her, he would see to it that she went up in flames.

Whatever happened next, at least she could finally say that she'd made love with a man who thoroughly satisfied her—repeatedly so, each time better than the time before.

No. Ella did not want this fling with Ian to end prematurely. She still had the rest of tonight and tomorrow to enjoy this beautiful, messed-up man. Time enough for regrets when they got home, time enough to pick up the pieces and figure out what came next.

"You're pissed at me," he said bleakly. "Aren't you?"

"Hmm." She pretended to have to think the question over. "Nope. Not pissed. Not in the least."

He tipped his head to the side, studying her, looking as though he didn't know quite what to make of her. "You're lying, right?"

"No, Ian. I am not lying. I'm not pissed. And as far as what's going on between you and your brothers and sisters, there's nothing wrong with how you feel. It's all new to you, what's happening this weekend. Be patient with yourself. The more you get to know them, the easier it will be to feel love for them."

He pursed up those lips that she couldn't wait to kiss again. "You assume that I *plan* to get to know them."

She gave a one-shouldered shrug. "I do, yes. I think you *will* get to know them. You just need the time to go about it in your own way."

"You're wrong."

She sucked in a calming breath and let it out slowly. "Ian. I have no desire to argue with you. I really don't. You'll figure it out is all I'm saying. Just give yourself a little space to get used to all the things that have happened over the past couple of weeks. The parts of your life that have been lost to you for two decades have come back to you. Nobody expects you to deal with all this instantly. Give yourself a break, why don't you?"

He made a face—something midway between a frown and a scowl. "You're too understanding, you know that?"

She snort-laughed. "So I've been told."

He let his chin drop and stared down at their half-eaten pizza.

"Go ahead," she whisper-teased, "have another slice. You know you want it."

He picked one up and stuck the end in his mouth, his blue eyes locked on hers as he chewed and swallowed. "I thought for a minute there that you would get up and leave."

"Nope. Still here."

"I wouldn't have blamed you. I'm a pain in the ass."

"Yeah, you kind of are."

"How'd I get so lucky to have you for a friend?"

"Life is full of great mysteries."

"Thanks." He took another bite, his brow crinkled in a frown.

She couldn't stop herself from asking for clarification, "And do you mean that thanks sincerely or with sarcasm?"

"Sincerely, Ell. I am completely sincere."

"So then, thanks for all the amazing advice, you mean?"

"Yeah, and all the ledges you seem to keep talking me down from—and especially for coming with. I couldn't do this without you."

"You're welcome." She drank the last of her sparkling water and turned to set the can on the nightstand. "What now?"

A slow, bad-boy grin spread over that too-handsome face. "I'm going to finish this slice and then get to work convincing you that you really need to take off my shirt."

Ian couldn't remember ever having as much fun with a woman as he'd had with Ella this weekend—in bed, and out of it, too. He'd always had a good time with Ell. But getting naked with her had somehow taken the fun to a whole new level.

That night and the next morning when he woke up beside her, he couldn't help thinking that the weekend wouldn't be enough. He needed more nights with Ella in his bed. They should talk about that.

But why waste a moment of their final day at the Isabel Inn renegotiating their sexual relationship?

Later for that. Today, he just wanted to enjoy every minute with her.

Sunday morning, they used two more condoms before breakfast. While using the second one, she screamed his name loud enough that he had to cover her mouth for fear the front desk would call and demand that they keep the noise down.

A little later, over French toast in the dining room, they discussed ways they might spend their final day in Oregon.

She asked, "Anything feel…incomplete?"

Leave it to Ella to ask the deep questions. "What does that even mean?"

"With your siblings? Anything you want to clear up with one of them, or *say* to one of them?"

"Wait." He set down the slice of bacon he'd almost stuck in his mouth. "You're asking if I need to spend more time with one of the Bravos before we fly home?"

"Yes, I am. Meeting your long-lost family, that's what you're here for. If there's any unfinished business, why not deal with it now?"

Unfinished business…

The two words, which had suddenly grown sharp edges, bounced around in his brain.

He thought of Matthias, of the look on Matt's face when they spoke up at Daniel's house during the big reunion dinner Friday night, of the feeling he'd had that Matt blamed himself for what had happened the day that Finn Bravo wandered away from his family and didn't come back until twenty years later.

Yeah. He probably should spend some time with Matt.

He didn't want to, though. He wanted a whole day with Ella, just the two of them. Before they had to return to their real lives, before he needed to figure out if he could stand to go back to being just friends again so soon—not to mention, whether she would even be open to the idea of continuing their arrangement for a while.

He feared she wouldn't. He'd gotten unbelievably lucky to get these few days with her this way.

And that made every minute they had together today even more important.

The way he saw it, if Matt had needed to talk about what went down all those years ago, wouldn't he have brought it up Friday night—or yesterday, for that matter?

"No." He picked up the slice of bacon he'd

dropped and popped it in his mouth. As soon as he'd swallowed it, he added, "I've got no unfinished business with any of the Bravos. I'm good."

Her eyes said she didn't believe him. But she let it go. "There's a rack of brochures at the front desk. We can pick the best local attractions and play tourist for a day."

"As long as we put aside plenty of time to be naked, I'm fine with that."

She sipped her coffee. "Lately, you seem a little obsessed with sex, don't you think?"

"Along with being a hair pervert?"

"Yeah, that, too. Maybe you should get help."

"I don't need help. I just need more time in bed with you."

She dragged a final bite of French toast in the puddle of marionberry syrup still on her plate. "Okay, then. You got it. We'll see the sights."

"And have the sex."

She groaned around the bite of French toast. "You're gross."

"Eat your bacon, too. You're going to need the energy when I get you alone back in the room."

Ian's phone chimed with a text as they walked to the room. They paused in the hallway and he checked the message, his gut kind of sinking at the inevitability of the moment as he saw who it was. "Matt wants to talk to me."

Ella didn't seem the least surprised. "He lives up by Astoria, right? Are you going to meet him at his farm?"

"Actually, he's here. In the parking lot." Ian stuck the phone back in his pocket.

"Perfect. I'll grab my purse and get scarce. You guys can have the suite to yourselves." She started walking again.

He caught her arm and pulled her back. "Hold on. What are *you* going to do?"

She gave an airy wave. "Don't worry about me. I'll walk on the beach or see what's on offer at the spa—and don't forget you did sign me up to drive the Lexus. Give me the keys. I'll grab a brochure and check out downtown Valentine Bay or whatever. It's not a big deal. You can just text me when Matt leaves."

"I'm sure it won't be long." The shorter the better, as far as he was concerned.

Now she turned fully toward him. Her soft hand brushed his cheek. "Take your time. I mean it." She lifted that mouth he couldn't get enough of, and they shared a quick kiss. Her lips tasted of rich coffee and sweet, tart berries.

He let her go reluctantly.

* * *

A few minutes later, Ella left him alone in the suite.

Too soon, the tap came at the door. He answered and found himself looking into blue eyes a lot like his own. They were about the same height and build, him and Matt. Same dark gold hair, too. Stepping back, Ian signaled his brother inside.

Matt stuck his hands in the pockets of his field jacket and stayed on the threshold. "Thanks for seeing me."

"No thanks needed. It's good," he lied outright, "for us to get a chance to talk alone."

"Ella?"

"She took the keys to the rental car. No doubt she's about to go wild in the streets of Valentine Bay."

That brought a reluctant smirk from Matt. "I'll bet."

They stood there, still as matching statues on either side of the door, staring at each other. Finally, Ian said, "You planning on coming in?"

Matt stared at him, a stare full of pain and something else. Guilt, maybe? He still had his hands in his jacket pockets. "I was thinking maybe a walk down on the beach…"

* * *

Ian put on a light jacket and ushered Matt through the sitting area and out to the deck.

Neither of them spoke as they went down to the cliff and from there took the second, longer set of stairs to the sand. Once on the beach, Ian slipped off his shoes and socks. Matt headed for the ocean in his heavy, lace-up boots.

At the water's edge, they turned south toward the headland, the same way Ian and Ella had gone Friday morning, when she'd talked him out of running away. Matt remained silent as they walked. Fine with Ian. Meaningless chatter didn't thrill him in the least.

The bench-like sea stack Ian remembered remained clear of the water. He and Matt sat there, just as he and Ella had done.

Matt stared off toward the distant horizon for a while. Ian felt no urge to start yakking. He figured Matt would start talking when he was damn good and ready.

And he did, turning his head toward Ian, giving him another wry sort of smile. "You used to be a talker."

He remembered, but he kept his mouth shut and gave his brother a nod of encouragement.

Matt took his silence exactly as Ian had meant him to—as a cue to go on. "Everything was a big thrill to you. And everything that thrilled you, you talked about. Incessantly. The day you disappeared, I was pissed off. I was fourteen and way too cool to be traipsing around Russia with the family. I wanted to be home in Valentine Bay with my buds like any normal teenage boy..." Matt's voice trailed off. He stared out at the ocean again.

After a minute or two, he went on, "We took a day trip on dog sleds from Irkutsk. You disappeared when we stopped for lunch. The way it happened, I went off across the snow on my own, wanting to be left alone to sulk. You followed me, chattering away a mile minute, as you always did. I turned on you. I yelled at you to shut the hell up. I think I scared you, freaked you out. Because after that, I never heard another sound from you. I turned my back on you and started walking again. Not once did I check on you, not even a single, quick glance over my shoulder. Not for way too long.

"Eventually, your silence started nagging at me. I did look back. You weren't there. I shrugged it off, assuming you'd rejoined the others. By the time I trudged back to the sleds to get something to eat, you'd been gone for maybe half an hour..." He fell silent again.

Ian waited him out.

Finally, Matt said, "The mushers knew how to

track. They should have been able to find you. But somehow, you'd vanished into thin air." He faced Ian again and said flatly, "So yeah. It was me. My fault. Everything that happened to you, all that you lost. All that you suffered. I did that to you because I was a spoiled, thoughtless boy without the sense God gave a goat."

Ian shook his head.

Matt glared. "What's that? What does that *mean*?"

"It means no, you didn't do it to me."

Now Matt did look pissed. "I was there. I know what happened."

"So was I. And I do, too. I don't remember everything, but I remember that day. I remember how it happened."

"Then you remember it wrong. I yelled at you. I told you to stop talking. And you did."

"Yeah. I remember that. I remember why you got on my case, how I babbled away about wanting a husky and talking Mom into getting me one. I remember you yelling at me—and I remember shutting up, trudging along behind you, thinking bad thoughts about you for a few minutes, maybe five, tops. But I got over it. I wasn't mad anymore when I wandered off."

Matt muttered, "You're just trying to make me feel better."

"I'm just trying to tell you that it wasn't your fault. I didn't wander off because you were mean to me. I saw a white chipmunk and followed it."

"A white…?"

"They're native to Siberia. Look it up. When the chipmunk got away from me, I heard a rustling in the underbrush. I ran to check that out—and found exactly nothing. From there, I spotted a quail, I think. I ran after it. I saw something glitter in the snow, but when I got to it, there was nothing. It went on like that. I was eight in a strange land, eight and curious—and fearless, too. Up till then, nobody had ever hurt me. As a rule, I could talk my way out of just about anything."

"Yeah," Matt agreed wryly. "Mom and Dad always claimed they never played favorites. But somehow, you always managed to get them to let you do just about whatever you wanted to do."

"Exactly. Curious, fearless and dangerously overconfident. I was chasing after nothing, living this big adventure inside my own head. It was probably an hour, at least, from the time I veered off the trail behind you until I started to realize I didn't have a clue where I'd wandered off to."

Matt wasn't buying. "It was my job to keep track of you."

"You went for a walk by yourself. Nobody told you to watch me. Before Mom let me take off after you, she gave me instructions to stay with you. I put on my most serious, well-behaved face and promised I would stick right by you. It's no more on you what happened than it is on me."

They both fell silent. Ian enjoyed the sound of the waves, thinking that this conversation had made him feel closer to Matt, more immediately connected to the childhood he'd only recently begun to recall. He thought about what Ella had said the night before, how as time went on, he would grow to care about these people who had turned out to be his family. Sitting here on the sea stack next to Matt, watching the gulls over the water as the morning fog thinned and the day started to warm up, Ian could almost understand what Ella had been trying to get through to him.

When they started back toward the inn, Matt said, "I just wanted to tell you how sorry I am, to let you know that I screwed up in a big way and I never really forgave myself for what happened that day."

Ian hardly knew how to answer him. "I get it, why you feel that way. If you need my forgiveness, it's yours, man. Whatever makes it better for you. I don't blame you, though. I never did. Because it wasn't your fault."

A humorless chuckle escaped the man beside

him. "I thought you'd only recently started remembering what happened."

"A couple of weeks ago, yeah—so you're right. For two weeks, I haven't blamed you. For the last couple of decades, I didn't have a clue what happened, anyway."

When they got back up the stairs to the cliffs above the beach, Ian asked, "Want coffee? We can go to the dining room."

Matt followed him through the suite and down the outside hallways to the round restaurant at the center of the inn. They had coffee and talked some more—about the farm where Matt lived with his wife and baby son, about his job as a game warden. He said he liked working outdoors, not being tied to a desk.

"So...you and Ella?" Matt asked when the server had refilled their cups for the second time. As Ian tried to decide how exactly to answer the not-quite question, Matt added carefully, "You two seem close."

Ian shrugged. "We are. She started at Patch&Pebble nine years ago, when she was still at NYU. We've been friends almost since her first day as an intern. Her daughter, Abby, and I are close, too. Abby's something special. She's eleven now."

Matt eyed him sideways. "I know it's none of

my damn business, but I gotta say it. Just friends? Not really buying that one."

Ian made a bad joke of it. "Didn't I just say she's eleven?"

Matt scoffed. "You know I'm not talking about the daughter."

Ian wanted to insist, *We are just friends.*

However, there was no *just* about what he had with Ella. She mattered to him in a big way.

As for having her in his bed, nothing compared. He felt far from ready to give that up, though the more he thought about it, the more he knew he needed to stick with the original plan.

No matter how much he craved her, he had to face facts. Ella wanted love and forever, and he simply didn't.

Nothing good could come of continuing this way. Too many things could go wrong.

Not that Matt needed to hear any of that.

"Truth is, Ell's my *best* friend. I don't know what I would do without her."

Matt shook his head. "It's strange, you know? I want to give you some good advice because you're my little brother. But on the other hand, you're also Ian, and I've only known you since Friday."

"Let me be succinct. Don't."

Matt threw back his head and let out a laugh. "Now how did I know you were going to say that?"

* * *

Surprise, surprise. The shops in the Valentine Bay Historic District didn't open until eleven on Sundays.

But Ella got lucky, because the Valentine Bay Sunday Market, which claimed a couple of streets and a big parking lot not far from the Valentine Bay Theatre, opened at nine. Ella browsed the booths that sold everything from wine to flowers to cute wooden birdhouses and chain-saw art. The food options were endless and the atmosphere nothing short of festive.

She bought some pretty beaded silver bookmarks and a handmade bracelet for Abby. The bookmarks really charmed her, so she went back and purchased several more for Chloe and her girls, for Marisol and Charlotte, and for the girls at the office, too. An hour passed. She enjoyed herself, chatting up the booth owners, accepting business cards from half of them.

After she wandered out of the market, she ended up strolling down Manzanita Avenue, stopping to look in shop windows, thinking that Ian's visit with Matthias must have gone well. More than two hours had passed since she left the inn. No way Ian would put up with anyone for two hours unless he considered the time well spent.

She stood outside Valentine Bay Books, window shopping the reading options, thinking that the store might open before Ian called to say Matthias had left, when her phone pinged with a text.

From Ian.

Where are you? Come back now.

She laughed as she read it. The text was so very Ian. He wanted her back there, and he wanted her there now.

And oh, did she want to be there. With him.

Standing at the bookstore window, she started to text him back, to give him a little grief for his extreme curtness, when her fingers stopped working and she almost dropped the phone.

Because...

She couldn't wait to get back to him.

She couldn't wait to be near him.

Inside the cage of her chest, her heart went crazy. It ached. It pounded. It soared.

All her denials fell away. All her reasons why this couldn't happen to her, why she had more sense than that...it all just went up in smoke. All her excuses, her maybe-nots, her vows that no way would she be that foolish...

They all deserted her.

She couldn't lie to herself any longer.

That bitch Lucinda had it right. Her dear friend Marisol had told her the truth.

For the first time in her life, Ella knew what it felt like to be hopelessly in love.

She, Ella Haralson, who damn well ought to know better, had fallen in love with Ian McNeill.

Chapter Ten

"Focus," she muttered under her breath.

And how pitiful was that?

Now she was talking to herself.

Ell? You there?

"Answer him. You need to answer him…"

Swiftly, she thumbed out the simplest response.
On my way.

As she made the short drive back to the inn, her
every nerve humming, her heart full of yearning
and her mind a bowl of mush, she somehow managed to come to a decision.

She would play it by ear.

They had till tomorrow morning as temporary lovers. After that, as per their agreement, they once more became Ian and Ella, good buddies and colleagues.

With maybe some overlap tomorrow, during the drive to PDX and the flight back home...

She turned into the parking lot at the Isabel Inn and nosed the Lexus into a space not far from their suite. Shifting into Park and switching off the engine, she flopped back against the seat and let out a groan at the headliner.

Overlap? Seriously? As if they might sneak in a quickie on the road or in the air?

Mush. No doubt about it. Love had turned her perfectly functioning brain to pure goo.

Today and tonight. That would be all. Done. Finished. End of story.

Tomorrow, they would once again become Ella and Ian, just good friends.

Unless, the voice of her braver self whispered in her ear—unless she grew a pair and asked for more.

That could bring crushing disappointment with a dash of pure humiliation—and who did she think she was kidding? Not *could*. Uh-uh.

Asking for more most likely *would* get her the answer Ian gave to all his girlfriends: no.

Ian McNeill was not, nor had he ever been, open to more with a woman. He'd made that so very clear with every girlfriend he'd ever had in all the years she'd known him. And if his actions weren't enough to convince her, what about his warnings before he first took her in his arms? *I get bored,* he'd said. *I shut down, and I just want whoever she is this time gone.*

She winced at the thought of being *whoever she is this time.* She couldn't bear that, to watch him turn away, to hear him say he felt nothing and he wanted her to leave.

And yet…

How could she expect to claim the love she longed for if she couldn't even step up and tell the man what she felt in her heart?

Nothing ventured, as the old saying went.

"Think about it. Just give yourself some time and think about it," she whispered at the windshield.

Because yeah. She was talking to herself again.

Gathering her bags of Sunday Market finds off the passenger seat, she left the car and headed for the room. At the door to the suite, she waved her key card at the PIN pad. As the green light came on, Ian pulled the door open from the inside.

"There you are." He grabbed her arm and wrapped her up in his arms, crushing her bags of goodies between them.

She laughed up at him, thinking how beautiful he was, knowing she couldn't do it, couldn't ask him for more. She already knew his answer, and she just couldn't bear to hear it.

So she teased, "You must be glad to see me." She could feel the evidence of his happiness pressing, hard and ready, against her belly.

"You have no idea." And he kissed her. A long one, deep and wet, with serious tongue. The bags dropped to the floor right there by the door. Ian eased her purse off her shoulder. It followed the bags, hitting the tile with a loud plop.

And then he grabbed her hand and pulled her to his bedroom.

They fell across the bed, tearing at each other's clothes as they went down, both of them achieving complete nakedness in record time. He had the condom out of the wrapper and rolled on his hard length so fast, she hardly knew he'd done it.

But then she looked down between their bodies and saw him wrapped and ready. "Come here."

She pulled him close, twining her legs around him good and tight, moaning in bliss as he filled her.

"So good," he whispered against her parted lips.

"Yes" was the only word she knew.

They moved together, chasing completion, almost rolling off the mattress at one point, laughing about it, laughter that caught on deep, hungry groans.

So what if she would never have more from him? This, right this minute, her arms and legs wrapped tightly around him as he moved within her...

It wasn't love for him. She knew that. It wouldn't last past tomorrow morning.

But from now until then, she would cherish every moment.

There would be time later to cry over what she'd never have with him, time to deal with her own cowardice at the prospect of showing him her heart.

In the late afternoon, they put on minimal clothing and ordered a picnic-basket lunch from the dining room. Spreading the picnic blanket on the living area rug, they sat cross-legged on either side of the blanket to enjoy the feast. As they ate, Ian explained how it had turned out with Matt.

"It's good, I think," she said when he'd finished

the story. "Really good. I mean, it sounds like he was pretty messed over by your disappearance, and you got a chance to help him see what happened through your eyes, to realize he wasn't at fault." She high-fived him.

He laughed. "Only you give high fives for a good conversation."

"It's obvious to me that Matt needed to hear what you had to say. I think you took a crushing weight off his shoulders."

"Well, not completely. I think he still feels it all could have gone differently if he'd just kept an eye on me."

"Yeah, but you showed him that *you* don't blame him. That matters, Ian. That's important, and I'm so glad you were able to say that to him."

He reached across their living-room picnic to guide a lock of hair behind her ear. "What would I do without you?" He bent close and kissed her.

I love you. You're the one for me. There'll never be anyone else like you, Ian...

The words begged to be said. And she almost let them out.

But then he kissed her again, and she focused on that, on right now, on every moment they had left to be lovers three thousand miles from home in this gorgeous little town where he'd been born.

* * *

All the rest of that afternoon and into the evening, Ian couldn't stop thinking about changing the rules and extending this mind-blowing thing between them, taking it on home, playing it out all the way.

But that path would too likely only lead to trouble.

And he couldn't afford the risk—not with Ella. She meant too much to him. If it got messy when it ended, he would never forgive himself.

He never should have started this.

And yet, he couldn't make himself regret a single moment.

He just needed to let it end as planned. And he would—tomorrow when they headed home.

Their flight, with one stop in Minneapolis–St Paul, would leave Portland at eight fifteen in the morning, so they would need to get going well before dawn.

He didn't sleep well. And when she turned over at 3:00 a.m. and he saw her eyes flutter open, he reached for her. She went into his arms one more time. He made it last, memorizing every sigh, every naughty word and throaty moan. He drank in the feel of her all around him, taking him, owning him. He'd never been owned before, probably never would be again.

He reassured himself it was okay, that he could let her go, that he would still have her the way he always had—as his best friend.

Sometimes a man had to measure the risk, see the danger ahead and pull back from the brink.

At least that's what he told himself as they packed up to leave at a little past four.

Chapter Eleven

During the trip home, Ella tried hard to believe they could go back to what they'd had before.

But trying hard couldn't make them effortlessly best friends again. She reassured herself that eventually, they would get there. Eventually, her heart would stop aching.

Ian spent most of the flight on his laptop as she pretended to deal with messages on her phone. Later, she put on her sleep mask, turned her head to the window and closed her eyes. She slept fitfully. Beside her, he said nothing. When she gave up trying to sleep, the silence between them continued.

They had a car waiting at JFK. It took an hour and a half to get to her place. When the driver finally stopped across the street from her building, Ian started to get out to help her with her bags.

"Stay there," she said quickly, as the driver got out to take her bags from the trunk. "I can manage, no problem."

"Ell, I don't mind—"

"Of course you don't, but it's almost eight at night. I know you want to get home." He had a beautiful two-thousand-square-foot loft in Tribeca, even closer to the office than her co-op.

"Come on, it's ten minutes to my place. I'll help you upstairs first."

"Don't be silly. I've got it."

He looked at her so strangely. "What's the matter?"

"Nothing." She put on a too-big smile. "See you tomorrow."

"Ell…" He seemed not to know how to continue.

And she didn't want him to continue, anyway. Sheesh. They reminded her of that ancient, depressing Simon and Garfunkel song that her aunt Clara used to love, all "dangling conversation" and "superficial sighs."

"Tomorrow," she repeated unnecessarily and shut the door before he could say anything else.

At the rear of the car, she thanked the driver and tucked a twenty into his hand.

Footsteps pounded on the hardwood floor inside as she let herself in her apartment door.

"Mom!" Abby, dimples on full display, came racing at her down the long hall from the living area. "Surprise!" She threw herself at Ella.

With the door open and her bags waiting behind her, Ella spread her arms to gather her daughter in. They hugged each other tight. Ella breathed in the scent of Prada Candy, Abby's favorite perfume, and felt a little better about everything. If she couldn't have the man she loved, at least she had Abby to come home to.

Ella took her by her slender shoulders and held her away. "You're here all alone?"

Abby nodded. "We saw when your flight landed. Dad walked me over here. I was only here like ten minutes before you came."

"But I thought you were staying at your dad's tonight."

"I was, but Dad said it was okay to come on over."

"Of course it's okay. It's more than okay. I'm glad you're here."

"Good. 'Cause I couldn't wait to see you— where's Ian?" Abby craned her head around Ella to peer out the open door to the hallway. "Is he coming up?"

Just the mention of his name caused a tightness in Ella's chest. But she kept her smile in place. "He went on home."

Abby caught both her hands. "Well, come on. Let's get your suitcases in. Did you eat?"

Ella almost burst out crying—partly in mourning for her too-brief love affair with Ian. But also for happiness, that she had a beautiful, thoughtful daughter who loved her. The teen years loomed ahead, and things would no doubt get rocky. But right now, Abby was a total sweetheart, and Ella felt like she'd hit the jackpot as a mom.

"Mom," Abby prompted. "I asked if you ate?"

"I had something on the plane."

"Okay. You can make some coffee or tea or whatever and tell me all about Ian's long-lost family and Valentine Bay."

Ian's loft had big windows. A lot of them.

That evening, he unpacked quickly, poured himself a whiskey and stood between the sofa and a giant potted umbrella tree to stare out at Lower Manhattan.

His place had never felt so big and empty.

Like some lovesick clown, he missed Ella already. She could've at least let him help her with her suitcases, let him come up for a few minutes. They could've had a drink, talked a little.

Even if he couldn't put his hands all over her, he'd always liked talking to her. They'd never had a shortage of things to say—not until today, anyway.

She'd hardly looked at him during their flights or during the stopover at MSP. And when she did look at him, she either smiled too wide or quickly glanced away.

Things would get better, though, he told himself. He just needed to give it time, and they would get back to their familiar, comfortable relationship.

Except…

Well, he still wanted her.

He wanted her a lot. Getting back to BFF status with her wouldn't help him with the wanting.

Not in the least.

That night, he didn't get a whole lot of sleep. More than once, he drifted off and woke up soon after. He lay there awake in the dark for way too long, wishing he had Ella in the bed beside him.

Tuesday came eventually. And it could've been worse—or so he told himself. He had meetings all day, which kept his mind occupied.

Unfortunately, a couple of those meetings included the COO who had kept him awake half the night. At least twice in both meetings she attended, he completely lost track of the topic, let alone what might have been decided. He nodded a lot and said, "That works," way too many times.

His gaze wouldn't stop straying her way. Today, she had all that amazing coffee-colored hair piled up in a loose knot at the top of her head. Little tendrils of the silky stuff had escaped. They kissed her temples and curled loosely down the nape of her neck.

He longed to get up and take the chair next to her, to lean in close, smell her perfect scent of coconut and spice, spear his fingers in that topknot, make it give way so he could wrap his hand around a giant hank of it. Once he had a good grip on all that silky hair, he would pull her good and close, take her mouth and not let go...

Yeah. He had no idea what had transpired in the meetings they had together. Yet somehow, he got through the day.

That night, he had drinks with two bachelor friends he'd known since they all went to Columbia together. They met up at a West Village tavern for burgers and beers. The place was packed with good-looking people, half of them female. More than one pretty woman came by their booth to chat.

His friends had fun. Neither went home alone. With a little bit of effort, Ian could have hooked up with someone new.

But that just felt all wrong. Hookups had never been his style. If he suddenly decided to go home with a stranger, it wouldn't be because he enjoyed that sort of thing.

Uh-uh. He would do it to try to get past how much he still wanted Ella.

As if such a move would even work. He knew ahead of time that it wouldn't. He would just end up feeling like crap about it—inviting some unknown woman home, using her to keep himself from knocking on Ella's door.

No unknown woman could distract him from what he wanted.

His needs were specific. All his fantasies involved Ella.

Why couldn't he stop thinking of her?

Easy. They'd had three days together. No way could that be called long enough for him.

He needed more. He needed the thing between them to play itself out. He needed dates with her, weekend getaways, a real relationship for as long as it lasted.

Too bad that, even inside his head, what he needed sounded selfish and completely unfair to Ella.

What did she need with him "for as long as it lasted"?

Really, she seemed to have moved on already.

She certainly hadn't expressed any interest in bringing their sexual relationship home with them from Oregon.

No. Asking for more just wouldn't cut it.

He needed to get over her.

And he would. He had to accept, though, that getting over her might take a while, because he'd lost her too soon, before he was ready.

But one way or another, this feeling of needing her, of longing to touch her, to kiss her, to hold her...

Eventually, the longing and needing would go away.

He only had to wait it out.

Wednesday, in a secure email, he received the DNA results Uncle Percy had arranged for. The results held no surprises. Daniel Bravo was his brother. And that made it official—he had a whole bunch of family in Valentine Bay.

Five minutes after he read those results, at a little after noon Eastern time, the calls started. He heard from every one of his siblings in Oregon—beginning with Madison the movie star, who sounded tired but happy. Madison explained that at 6:43 a.m. Pacific time, she'd given birth to a seven-pound, ten-ounce baby girl. Madison and

Sten had named the little one Evelyn Daffodil, after Sten's mother and Aunt Daffy.

"Of course, we're calling her Evie already," Madison added with obvious pride.

"It's a beautiful name," said Ian, feeling oddly bewildered. For so much of his life, he'd had only Glynis. Now he had brothers and sisters and nieces and nephews, so many he had trouble keeping them all straight.

He'd barely hung up from Madison when Daniel called. Matt called while Ian was still on with Daniel, so Ian called him back as soon as he and Daniel said goodbye.

"Hello, little brother," said Matt. "It's hardly a surprise that you're a Bravo, but it's fun welcoming you to the family all over again. We're all really hoping you can make it for Hailey's wedding at the end of the month—and as long as we're talking weddings, there's also Gracie and Dante's wedding in mid-June. It's a lot to ask, we know. But think about maybe flying out for both."

Ian stifled a groan. Both Daniel and Madison had mentioned Hailey's wedding. Ian had said both times that he would try. Now he had Gracie's big day to think about, too? He said it again, "I'll see what I can do."

"Can't ask for more."

Ian's phone lit up with a call from Connor. He

said goodbye to Matt and got on the line with his second-born brother.

By the time every one of his siblings—*and* Percy *and* Daffodil—had expressed their joy and excitement at the news that wasn't really news to anyone, Ian felt relief that all the calls had finally been made.

He also felt a little, well, happy. The Bravos were good people. And as usual, Ella had gotten it right.

He'd always considered himself content not knowing where he'd started out, always told himself that he'd gotten everything that really mattered when Glynis adopted him, that she was all the family he'd ever needed.

But the mystery of his past had always haunted him, no matter how hard he'd tried to deny that it did.

He had a feeling some of the holes in his memory would never fill in. It felt good, though, to know that Finn Bravo had started out his life loved and cared for. That he'd *mattered* to his family, that they'd looked for him and never stopped.

And slowly, as he got over the shock of their very existence, he found he had good feelings when he thought of them, a certain gladness that they existed, that they really seemed to want to include him in their family events whenever possible.

Yeah.

Ella was right. In time, he could definitely get used to having a big family.

He went to her office and found the door wide open. She stood beside her desk, typing something on her phone, looking amazing in a soft white shirt and pink pencil skirt, sky-high nude heels on her slender feet.

"Hey." He tapped on the door frame.

She looked up. For a moment, they simply stared at each other. He imagined himself crossing the threshold, kicking the door shut as he entered, marching straight to her, grabbing her close and crashing his hungry mouth down on hers.

In real life, he stayed right where he was.

She set the phone down and smiled—a forced smile. "Hey."

He leaned in the doorway and drank in the sight of her—right here at Patch&Pebble, a single wall between his office and hers. So close.

And yet a million miles away.

"I got my DNA results a little while ago," he said.

As he rambled on about all the calls from Oregon, her face relaxed a little and her forced smile turned real. "I'm so glad, Ian. You're fortunate to have such a wonderful family."

"Yeah," he said quietly. "I wanted to tell you that I'm starting to see what you meant, about how it would take time, but I would slowly realize how good it is to know them, to start to see them as an important part of my life."

She gave him a slow nod—of acknowledgment, of understanding.

But then he suggested, "Want to run out for some lunch? How about that place around the corner we both like?"

She was already shaking her head, that invisible wall between them going up again, cutting him off from her. "Samar's ordered takeout." Samar was her assistant. "I've got a video conference with Production."

He felt so bad—exiled, displaced. Banished.

From Ell, of all people. He'd lost his best friend when he took her to bed. He could kick his own ass for his own total foolishness. And yet, at the same time, he knew damn well that given the chance, he would do it—do *her*—all over again.

In a heartbeat if she would let him.

Right then, he despised himself. He'd lost his best friend for a weekend fling.

All the good family feeling of a minute ago deserted him, left him empty, lurking in her door-way, with nothing else to say.

"Fair enough. I'll leave you to it." And he turned and started walking, marching right past his office, headed for the elevator. As he passed Audrey's desk, he said, "Back in an hour."

His assistant smiled and then frowned. He just kept walking, his mind lost in Ella, wishing…

But it didn't matter what he wished, now did it?

He needed to get over wanting her. And then, eventually, he would have his friend back. The old ease and companionship would be his again.

He refused to consider that it might go any other way.

Thursday, Ella had lunch with Marisol—a lunch during which she promised herself she would *not* bring up the subject of Ian.

They met at a small Italian restaurant they both liked on Ninth Avenue, where they served wine by the glass and delicious prosciutto and mozza-rella sandwiches.

Marisol breezed in, her cloud of natural curls bouncing, her dewy amber skin aglow. "Love the gorgeous bookmarks," she said. Ella had given them to Abby to give to Charlotte. "Thank you," Marisol said as soon as they had their wine.

"I'm so glad you like them. They have a great

little farmers market there in Valentine Bay. The chain-saw art alone left me breathless. I mean, a life-size, anatomically correct bull moose? It almost killed me not to bring that one home."

"And yet somehow, you restrained yourself?" Marisol teased.

"I did, yes."

Marisol allowed only a few seconds to elapse before demanding, "Oregon with Ian, huh? How did it go?"

Her chest too tight and her heart heavy, Ella turned her wineglass by the stem. "I take it Abby's been talking."

"She's eleven. Of course she's been talking. When I picked the girls up from hip-hop class Friday, she chattered the whole way to Philip's about Ian's newfound family. Then Monday, after tap class, she said you and Ian were coming home that night."

"Yeah. The trip was pretty tough for Ian..." Quickly, she filled her friend in on the parts of Ian's story that Marisol hadn't already heard.

Their sandwiches came. When the waitress left, Marisol kept after her. "But what about you? Wasn't it tough on *you*, to be there alone with him, supporting him as a friend, given the way that you feel?"

"The way that I *feel*?" Ella couldn't resist playing dumb on the love question. After all, she'd yet to admit to anyone but herself how she really felt about her friend and boss. "I have no idea what you're talking about."

"Oh, yes you do. Don't be coy. Be strong. Be true."

Should she keep her big mouth shut?

Hard yes on that.

But then again, she pretty much always told Marisol everything, and she did need to talk to a friend about this…

Marisol took a big gulp of wine. "Okay. I can't take it. Something happened. Tell. Me. Everything."

"Well, as I said, Ian was pretty tense the whole trip out there. Thursday night, he had a nightmare about the past. He cried out in his sleep. I went into his room to see if I could help. After I woke him up, we started talking…"

"And talking wasn't all that happened, right?"

Slowly, Ella nodded. "I stayed with him all night. The next day we came to an agreement to be together, to be lovers, but just for the time in Oregon."

"A fling."

"Yeah."

"And then?"

"It was beautiful. I loved every minute of it.

And by Sunday, I realized that you and that harpy Lucinda were right."

Marisol smirked. "You did it. You admitted you're in love with him."

"Could you not look so smug?"

Marisol waved her hand, long fingers spread, in a circle in front of her own face. "This is not my smug look. This look means 'It's about time.'"

With a hard sigh, Ella picked up her wine and downed a fortifying sip. She set the glass down firmly. "Yeah. I'm in love with him. I realize that now."

"Good. So then...what happened next?"

"Next? We kept the agreement. It's over. We came home."

"Oh, baby..." Marisol reached across their little table. Ella met her halfway, and they laced their fingers together. Marisol gave her a reassuring squeeze before they let go. She asked gently, "So then it went badly, when you told him that you love him?"

Ella had just picked up her sandwich for another bite. She set it back down.

And Marisol *knew*. She accused, "You haven't told him."

Ella stared glumly at her sandwich. "Are you *trying* to ruin my appetite?"

"Let me phrase that as a question. Have you told Ian that you love him?"

"I've thought about it. A lot."

Her friend reached for her hand again. She gave it. They leaned across the table, fingers intertwined.

Marisol said, "Sweetheart, you have to tell him."

"No, I don't."

"Oh, honey…" Marisol shook her curly head.

"It won't do any good. He doesn't want a relationship, ever. He said something shuts down in him after he's with someone for a while. He says he's just not going there. He says that love, marriage and all that are never going to happen for him."

"A lot of men say that—women, too—until they meet someone who makes them change their mind."

"I'll bet Jacob never said that. Your husband adored you at first sight. And the way you've always told it, you felt the same for him. So I'm asking you, what men? What women?"

"You just made my point. Jacob and I were right for each other, and we were fortunate that we both knew it from the start. Not everybody is like that. It takes some people longer to come to grips with their love. But they have to stay open to making it work. They have to be brave and up-front about what they want with the person they love—and you're not behaving bravely, Ella. You're not being up-front. You are evading."

"Gee, Mari. Tell me what you *really* think."

"I think you should tell him how you feel."

"I know you do. But you're not me. It was a simple thing for you, with Jacob, for both of you. You just now admitted that. With Ian, I'm fighting a losing battle."

"Uh-uh. Not true. Not necessarily—but okay, say you're right. Say Ian is the only guy in Manhattan who swears he'll never fall in love and settle down and means it. That doesn't change the fact that you need to tell the man you're in love with him. You need to do it for yourself, so that you will know you pulled out all the stops. That you put your whole heart in it, that he knows exactly what you want from him. How he takes it, what he does in response, that isn't the main issue."

"Maybe not to you. You're not the one who gets to face the rejection."

"You can't be sure he'll turn you down until you tell him what you want."

"Easy for you to say."

"You're right. It *is* easy for me to say. And I never said it would be easy for *you* to do. I said that you *need* to do it. You need to stand up for your heart and tell the man you're in love with him."

For Ian, the hits just kept coming—Ella-wise, anyway.

Not only was she missing from his bed now, she'd gone AWOL from their friendship, as well. From the moment they got in the car to head for the airport on Monday, she'd been distant with him.

She spoke to him only when necessary. If he walked into the break room, she walked back out again. On Friday, he tried harder to get her alone, to get her to talk to him, to look him in the eyes.

Really, would it kill her to give him a damn smile?

She had to walk by the open door of his office to get to hers. Friday morning, he watched for her.

Ten minutes after she zipped by, he went to her. At least she'd left her door ajar again. She sat behind her desk typing something on her MacBook.

He tapped on the door frame, just the way he had on Wednesday. "Got a minute?"

Her smile came fast—a cool smile that matched the distant expression on her beautiful face. "Sure. Come on in."

He shut the door behind him.

She bit her upper lip. He wished she'd let him do that.

But she wouldn't. Because that part of their relationship was through.

The rest of what they had, though? What about that? Didn't years of friendship matter? The more he thought about it, the less he liked her putting up a wall between them. So what if they'd had a hot weekend together? Why should that mean he had to lose her as his friend?

"What's up?" she asked him—not impatiently, exactly. But she had a vibe, that *how can I help you so you can leave?* vibe.

He forged ahead with an unnecessary question about the upcoming product launch of Woodrow the warthog.

"Sounds good to me," she said when he stopped talking. She was still smiling. Her big brown eyes asked, *Anything else?*

We weren't supposed to lose our friendship because we had sex, but it looks like we have. He should just say it, just ask her, *Have we lost our friendship?* But she looked so…unwelcoming.

Maybe if he got her out of the office. In a nonwork setting, they could talk honestly and frankly—about the fling, the end of the fling, what was going on with her now, all of it. "You free tonight?"

Something flashed in her eyes. It looked like panic. "No. Really. I have, um, stuff."

"Stuff?"

She threw her hands up, outright impatient now. "You know, *things* that I, uh, I need to do."

It was too much. He bent at the waist, braced his hands on her desk, leaned into her space and said quietly, "We need to talk. You know we do."

Two bright spots of color rode high on her soft cheeks, and her mouth drove him crazy. He almost lunged forward and claimed it with his. "Ian, I just don't—"

"Please. Let me come to your place. Or you come to mine. Go to lunch with me, whatever works for you."

She stared at him, stricken. And then she gulped. "Um. Okay."

He waited for her to name the place and time. When she just continued to stare, he did it for her. "Is Abby at her dad's for the weekend?"

She hard-swallowed again. "Yes."

"Your co-op, then. I'll be there at nine tomorrow morning."

Ella managed to avoid Ian for the rest of the workday.

At home, she felt desperate and lonely and wished Abby was there. Five times that evening, she almost called Ian and asked him not to come.

But no. He had a point. They needed to talk about this.

She needed to do what Marisol had challenged her to do—tell him she loved him and take it from there.

In bed, sleeping proved impossible. She spent half the night on her laptop watching decade-old episodes of *How I Met Your Mother* and *Scrubs*, shows she'd seen too many times already. Something about their familiarity soothed her somehow.

By 6:00 a.m., she couldn't stay in bed a minute longer. She got up, showered and dressed and then started cleaning things to keep busy. She dusted shelves and vacuumed rugs, and by seven thirty, she felt grubby and sweaty.

So she showered and changed clothes again. Piling her hair up in a casual knot, she refused to allow herself to spend more than ten minutes on minimal makeup. Marisol's advice kept playing in her brain on an endless loop.

...you need to tell the man you're in love with him. You need to do it for yourself, so that you will know you pulled out all the stops. That you put your whole heart in it, that he knows exactly what you want from him...

It sounded so good inside her head.

But the little girl from Oklahoma who'd lost her parents and suddenly found herself in an Upper

East Side apartment with an aunt who only took her out of duty—that unwanted little girl was still inside her, the same way the little boy torn from his family and lost in Siberia still lived inside Ian.

How could she and Ian ever get to love and forever together when he'd made it so clear that he would never even try?

They wrote songs and made movies about that, didn't they? How two people filled each other's gaps, fixed each other's broken places.

But movies and songs, they were just fantasies. In real life, it hurt so bad to be the one that nobody wanted. In real life, a woman could work on her confidence, make herself step up, put in the effort and time for her degree. She could divorce the nice guy and good friend she'd married at his parents' insistence—divorce him so that both of them could find the love of a lifetime. A woman could get a great job in a growing company, raise a beautiful, smart, kindhearted daughter, all while holding out for the one man, the *right* man.

And then, when said woman finally realized she'd found the man for her, it wouldn't matter. Not in the least. Because she'd chosen a man who didn't want a forever with anyone.

A long chain of obscene words scrolled through her brain.

It was all just so wrong.

She didn't want to be brave and strong and determined, damn it. Not about this.

Couldn't a man's love be the one thing in all her life that came easy? Couldn't the man she wanted be sure and strong in his heart? Couldn't her man be the one to say it first, the one to coax her along, to make the impassioned promises that they would work it out, that everything would be all right?

She stood at the window in the living area, staring blindly through the glass at the back of the Chelsea Hotel, thinking how she'd spent her life picking up the pieces, doing what she had to do to build a decent future. Thinking about how love had to go both ways, and with Ian, that would not be happening.

The more she stewed on it all, the more she wanted to pitch a toddler-worthy tantrum, maybe break a few dishes. She wanted to throw the window open, lean out with her hands on the sill and howl in frustration. Longed to scream out her hurt and anger loud enough that they would hear her cry all the way to the Hudson Yards.

The intercom buzzed. Ian had arrived.

And she was furious.

She marched to the door, buzzed him up and then stood there, waiting, every nerve in her body vibrating with frustration, until he knocked.

Ripping off the chain and slamming back the dead bolt, she yanked the door wide.

And there he stood, every woman's dream of male perfection, with his sexy blue eyes and thick, wavy hair, his broad shoulders and deep chest, that strangely compelling facial scar. He held a cardboard tray with coffees from the place up the street, a bakery bag dangling from one big hand.

They stared at each other. He looked vaguely alarmed at the sight of her. "Why are you mad?" he asked. Because of course, he knew her so very well.

He could know her a little less and unconditionally adore her a lot more. That would totally work for her.

"I'm fine," she said and ushered him in.

He followed her to the kitchen, where he set down the bag and coffees and turned to peer at her through narrowed eyes. "*Fine* is not a good word. Not when you have that expression on your face."

Violent urges quivered through her. She really needed to chill. So what if she loved him and he couldn't—or simply wouldn't—love her?

She'd always been the most reasonable person in any room.

Where had all her levelheadedness gone?

"I brought you a latte, one Splenda," he offered cautiously, like a zookeeper throwing fresh fish to a hunger-mad polar bear. "And a bagel, cream cheese and strawberry jam on the side, just the way you like it."

"Thank you." She gestured at the dining table behind them. "So...you want to sit?"

"Great." He said it kind of hopefully—but with an edge of desperation.

She reminded herself that he was trying. That he cared about her. That he clearly didn't want to lose her as a friend. Or as his COO.

She took the bakery bag and he took the coffees. He sat facing the window. She sat in the chair just around the corner from him, with a view of the bright room's brick accent wall and bookcases full of personal mementos, her favorite books and her daughter's, too.

She removed the lid from her latte and had a sip. "So good. Thanks."

He almost smiled as he sipped from his own cup.

A terrible thought occurred to her as she unwrapped her bagel.

Had he come here to tell her he couldn't work with her anymore?

The very idea had her fury escalating again. Seriously? The nerve of him if he did that. She did an amazing job for him, and she loved Patch&Pebble. They were a great team.

Or they always had been.

Possibly not so much this past week. He'd seemed a little distracted. And to be perfectly honest, she had been, too.

Her anger settled to a simmer. She felt marginally calmer.

It occurred to her then that changing jobs might be the answer for this problem she had. Having to see him every day—well, it was awful. She might get over him more easily if she didn't see him at all.

And it wasn't as if she lacked options. More than one other company had sent headhunters her way with excellent offers. And Ian paid her a top salary, with generous bonuses. She had a nice nest egg to tide her over should that become necessary.

It made her sad, though, to think of leaving the company. She'd never wanted a change. She loved her job and everything about it—or she had until recently.

And even if she left Patch&Pebble, she would probably still have to see him now and then. He and Abby shared a strong bond. He cared for Abby as much as he could care for anyone—so no, he wouldn't want to lose what he had with Abby. And it would hurt Abby if he vanished from her life.

But Ella could cope with occasionally having to see him for her daughter's sake. Dealing with him for a few minutes now and then wouldn't be near the hell she currently lived in, having to work with him every day.

"Something wrong with the bagel?" he asked.

She yanked her shoulders back and stared straight at him.

He said in a cautious tone, "You unwrapped it and then you just sat there, staring at it…"

She glanced down at the bagel, unwrapped, her hands on the table to either side of it, the little tubs of jam and cream cheese nearby.

So what if she'd only stared at it? She had bigger things on her mind than a bagel.

"It's fine," she replied through clenched teeth.

He muttered, "There's that word again."

She took the bagel by the corner of the open wrapper and pulled it out of her way. Then she braced her forearms on the table, folded her hands between them and stared him straight in the eye. "Listen. Can we just get down to whatever it is you wanted to talk about?"

He jerked up straight in his chair. It took her a moment to realize he looked absolutely terrified.

And just like that, in an instant, her fury at him melted away. Because she loved him, damn it. She couldn't stand being around him now. It hurt too much. But neither could she bear seeing him upset.

She ached to reach across the distance between

them, put her hand on his, ask him coaxingly, *What is it? What's wrong? How can I help?*

Somehow, she kept her hands to herself. Sucking in a deep breath to settle her churning emotions, she suggested softly, "Whatever it is, why don't you just tell me, just say it? I'll help in any way I can."

He glanced down at his untouched coffee and from there, out the window. Finally, he looked at her again. "I don't want it to be over with us," he said in a low, pained growl.

Her heart slammed against her rib cage, soaring, aching for him, expanding with hope. That he still wanted her.

That just maybe it wasn't over for him any more than it was for her.

She just needed to do it, like Marisol said. Just open her mouth and say that she loved him...

He said slowly, with care and intensity and passion, "I think we made a mistake, putting an artificial ending on it. I want to be with you, Ell. So much. For as long as it lasts."

As long as it lasts...

She drew in a slow breath and let it out with care.

No. Just no.

That wasn't good enough—oh, but that look in his eyes. It said so much more than his words.

That look said he wanted her, needed her, the same as she needed him. That he couldn't stop thinking about her, longing for her, reaching for her in the night…

And finding nothing but emptiness.

She stared into those beautiful eyes—and realized her throat had locked up tight from the pain and turbulence inside her. She swallowed, hard, to relax it.

And she made herself say what *she* needed from *him.* "You would have to agree to be open to, um, more."

More?

Oh, God. Could she be any wimpier?

"More?" He echoed the word, gruff and gentle at once—and wary now. He took her meaning. And he didn't feel the least comfortable with it.

Say it. Just get the damn words out. I love you, Ian. Do you—could you—love me, too? "Ian, come on, we've been friends forever. You know what I want. I want love and I want marriage. What happened in Oregon was beautiful. But I can't *not* be me. I can't go on with you unless you're willing to try to, um, be with me permanently."

Be with me permanently? Dear Lord have mercy. Had she really just said that?

Pathetic. Oh, yeah. That shrew Lucinda so had her pegged.

As for the handsome man around the corner of the table from her…

Silence. A long, awful stretch of endless, word-less seconds. He had that look, the one that spoke of regret and all the things he simply couldn't give her.

Finally, he said what she already knew he was thinking. "Ell. That would never work out."

She scoffed, softly. "In other words, no. You will never want to make it forever with me."

"You know me, Ell."

"Oh, yes, I do. And you know me." She stood, her heart twisting inside her chest, for what he re-fused to give. For the fact that she was losing him without ever having had him in the first place. "You really need to go, Ian."

"Yeah." He got up, too. Carefully, he pushed in his chair before he turned for the door.

She remained standing at the table, staring after him until he vanished down the hallway. A moment later, she heard the door click shut behind him.

Ella understood then. She knew what she had to do.

After reengaging the dead bolt and the chain, she got out her laptop and sent him an email.

From Ell's place Ian went straight to his gym. He stayed for three hours, lifting weights, working up a serious sweat on the elliptical machine, trying to burn off his misery and frustration. It didn't help much.

After a shower and lunch at a diner near the gym, he almost went back to his place. But the idea of sitting alone in his apartment wishing he were someone else so he could have Ella?

No, thanks.

He ended up walking to Battery Park and staring at the Hudson, then wandering around some more, taking the F train to Brooklyn Heights for no reason at all other than he needed to keep moving. He walked down to Cobble Hill and then up and down Court Street for a while before he finally got back on the subway and went home.

His apartment felt every bit as empty and lifeless as he'd known it would. He wandered from window to window, thinking about going out and getting drunk off his ass, knowing it was pointless. Getting plowed would only earn him a hangover.

It would take time, he kept telling himself. This obsession he had with his best friend would end eventually. They would get back to who they used to be together. His life would feel bearable again. He just had to wait it out.

And maybe stop acting like some hopeless, lovesick fool in the meantime. That wouldn't hurt.

Man up and stop dragging around like the world had come to an end.

Yeah. He would do that—buck up, get over himself.

Soon. Very soon…

He went to bed late and couldn't sleep. In the morning, he checked messages—and started to smile when he found an email Ella had sent yesterday, right after he left her co-op.

His smile died half formed as he read.

Ian,
Just a heads-up. Given the situation between us, I think it would be best if I left Patch&Pebble. I don't want to put you in a bind, so I'm happy to stay on for a few weeks to help train my replacement. I will visit HR to give my formal notice on Monday, so please let me know beforehand how long you'll need me to stay.
All best,
Ella

Through an enormous and heroic effort of will, he did not throw his laptop out the nearest window. Instead, for several minutes, he just sat there, fuming, debating the wisdom of going straight to her place all over again—this time to inform her that he would not accept her resignation.

Somehow, he quelled that wild impulse and replied reasonably and calmly to her email instead.

Ella,
You love your job. You've always sworn you would never work anywhere else. There's no reason to leave. Tell me you'll give it more thought before you make such an extreme decision.
Yours,
Ian

He hit Send and tried to concentrate on his other mail, though mostly he just stared at the far wall and considered whether he should go out for breakfast. It took about fifteen minutes for her reply to appear.

Ian,
I don't need to think about it. I've made up my mind. It's time for me to move on.

That did it. Enough of this email crap.

He grabbed his phone and called her.

She answered on the first ring. "Ian, it's what I want. You aren't going to change my mind. I'm happy to make it a smooth transition, but you need to tell me how long you'll—"

"Why, Ell? Just, honestly, why?"

She scoffed. "Please. You know why. We have to deal with reality."

"And that is?"

"It's no good between us now, okay?"

"*Okay?* What the hell? No, Ella. It's not okay. None of this is okay."

"I'm sorry you're upset about this, Ian, but—"

"You're damn right I'm upset. I get that you don't want to go on with me, that what happened in Oregon is as far as you're willing to go with me. I understand that. But eventually, things will get better. There's no reason to quit a job you love because we had a thing once for a few days."

"You're wrong."

"Ella, if you'd just—"

"No. Uh-uh. We never should have had a *thing*, as you call it. It was a bad idea for us to get into bed together. I never should have slept with you, but now that I have, I can't work with you. Not anymore."

"That makes no sense to me."

"Ian, it makes perfect sense."

"We can deal with your issues, whatever they are. You just need to tell me what's really bothering you. We'll work it out. We'll move on. As a team."

Dead silence on her end.

"Ella. Are you there?"

"I am, yes. And you're not listening to me. I am leaving Patch&Pebble. You need to hire someone else."

He couldn't let her do that. "No way. You're irreplaceable."

She scoff-laughed at that. "Please. I'm good, not irreplaceable. You'll find someone just as good. And since you seem so reluctant to decide how long you need me—"

"How can I decide that? I don't want you to go."

"But I am going. And since you won't name a date certain for my departure, I will do it for you. Three weeks and I am gone."

"Ella…" He struggled to find the words, the perfect words that would make her see that she really didn't want to quit.

She didn't wait for him to find those words. "I have to hang up now. Bye." The line went dead.

He started to call her back again, but sanity won out.

She meant it. She wanted out, and he couldn't stop her from going. Somehow, he would need to learn to live with that.

Ella was leaving Patch&Pebble.

And he had lost his best friend.

Chapter Twelve

Monday morning first thing, Ella turned in her formal resignation. And then she went to the morning meeting, dealt with a couple of crises in Minneapolis and touched base with the head of sales. David, their CFO, knocked on her door at noon.

"Lunch, Ella," he said. "Let's go. I'm buying." David had been at the company almost as long as Ella. She read his intention just from the look on his face.

"I'm leaving," she informed him. "I really am. You won't talk me out of it."

"Maybe not. But look at it this way—it's a free lunch, am I right?"

They went to a brasserie a couple of blocks away. David said how much everyone would miss her and he hoped she might consider changing her mind. She made it clear that her mind was made up.

"Well, I'm probably speaking out of turn," he said. "So shoot me. If you do change your mind, just be sure to let Ian know. You can always come back. You know that, right?"

"Did he ask you to say this?"

David chuckled. "I'm guessing you won't buy my act if I ask who you mean by 'he'?"

"I'm not coming back, period. Full stop."

"Aha. Say no more. You've made yourself perfectly clear."

"Good."

"Let's check out the dessert menu, shall we? I've heard the chocolate roulade is the stuff of dreams."

That afternoon, Ella arrived at the dance studio just as Abby and Charlotte's tap class ended. They rode the subway together, got off at Charlotte's stop and walked her to her building. From there, Ella and Abby walked the few blocks home. It was a perfect New York City evening, a few clouds drifting by way up there above the tops of the buildings, the temperature mild with a hint of a breeze. Ella focused on enjoying the moment, on clearing her mind of longing and sadness.

She'd decided to move on, and she'd made the right choice. It might take a while, but in time she would get over Ian. She had to. She saw no other option. What else could she do when the one she loved insisted he could never love her in return?

At home, Abby tossed a salad and heated garlic bread while Ella put together a simple pasta dish with sausage and marinara.

Abby seemed fine. She chattered about her day and got stars in her eyes over the Yankees home game Ian would take her to this coming Saturday against their century-long rivals, the Red Sox. Ella made the right noises in all the right places. She felt sure Abby had no idea that things had changed between Ella and Ian. Maybe she would get lucky—Abby would keep her own relationship with Ian and would never have to know that her mom's friendship with Ian had crashed and burned.

You just keep thinking that, scoffed a sour voice in her head.

Her daughter was no fool. Abby would figure it out even if no one ever told her the truth outright.

As soon as she found out that Ella had quit her job, Abby would know something had gone terribly wrong.

Ella's brilliant solution to that dilemma?

Put it off.

And she did, for three more days. By Thursday, she knew she had to get it over with. What if Ian said something on Saturday and she hadn't prepared Abby first?

No. She had to tell her daughter before Ian picked her up for the game. Either that or get Ian to agree not to mention anything about it.

But to get Ian to help her out with evading this issue she ought to just face, she would have to have a private conversation with him, one in which she asked for what could only be called a favor. She didn't feel comfortable asking Ian for favors, not the way things stood now.

And anyway, she avoided Ian as much as possible at work. He seemed to avoid her, too. They'd come to that. Putting up with each other. Both of them waiting out the time until they no longer had to deal with each other in any way, day to day.

No one at the office had said a word about her replacement. As far as she knew, they hadn't even started looking for anyone.

Not that it should matter to her. She would help however she could if asked. Otherwise, she just needed to get through the days until her last one.

Thinking of the mystery employee who would eventually take her place reminded her sharply that she needed to dust off her résumé. But she had enough money to get by for a while without much of a hit to her savings. A few weeks off wouldn't hurt her. She and Abby might go someplace tropical, take a little vacation, a break from real life.

Thursday night during dinner she spent several dreamy minutes picturing herself on a golden beach shaded by palm trees, at some luxurious resort where they offered any number of fun activities for the kids, while for sad, lovelorn single moms, they kept the umbrella drinks coming 24/7.

Abby said, "You're acting strange, Mom. You keep staring out the window, and when I ask you a question, you don't even hear me, and then I have to ask again before you give me an answer."

Realizing she couldn't put it off any longer, Ella said, "As a matter of fact, I am a little preoccupied, honey."

"Why?"

"I've decided on a career change. Two weeks from tomorrow will be my last day at Patch&Pebble."

Abby's mouth formed a large O. She blinked twice, after which she cried, "But you love your job. Why are you leaving?"

Busted. Clearly, she should have given this conversation careful forethought. However, too late now. She tried for an upbeat tone. "I just realized I'm ready for a change, you know?"

"No, Mom. I *don't* know." For a second or two, Ella braced for tears or accusations—or both. But then Abby drew a slow breath and tried to be calm. Ella loved her so much in that moment—loved both her passion and her true goodness of heart. "But, um, where will you be working now?"

"I'm not sure yet. I'm thinking of taking some time off. I'm thinking that as soon as school's out, you and I might take a little vacation."

"Yeah, but, Mom, I don't get it. What happened? Is something wrong? It does seem like something's been bothering you."

"Um, ahem. Well, of course it is a big change."

"Then why are you doing it? And wait a minute." Abby set down her fork. "Ian can't be happy about this. Is Ian okay?"

"Ian is fine."

Her daughter peered at her, brown eyes doubtful. "I can't see him being happy that you're leaving him."

Ella winced before she could stop herself. "Honey, I'm not *leaving* Ian. Not at all." Had her face turned red? That happened sometimes when she told a fib. She'd just never been all that good at lying—not that she'd lied just now.

She hadn't. Not exactly, anyway...

Abby's mouth had pinched up.

Guilt and misery flooded through Ella. Being

a mom? Hardest damn thing ever. How could she explain this to Abby honestly without saying way more than she should?

An eleven-year-old didn't need to know the gory details of a too-brief love affair gone sour. Especially not when the ex-lovers in question were her mother and the guy everyone called her second dad—the guy she'd known for years as her mother's best friend. To Abby, what went on between her mother and Ian had never gone beyond friendship. And the way Ella saw it, Abby never needed to know what had happened in Oregon.

Lord. It had been so much simpler when she and Philip had divorced. At two, Abby had taken the end of her parents' marriage in stride. She'd been too young to ask questions anyway, and Ella and Philip had never been at odds. Their relationship to each other had remained essentially the same— that of good friends with a daughter to raise.

Abby asked, "How many times have you said how much you love being part of creating the toys kids all over the world can't wait to call their own—and you also love working with Ian. Why would you ever give up what you love?"

Because I'm in love with Ian and he's not in love with me. Ella pressed her lips together to keep the bald truth from getting out.

She couldn't share that with Abby, couldn't take

the chance of damaging Abby's relationship with her second dad.

At the same time, Ella needed to help her daughter make sense of all this.

Ella decided to go with the truth, just easy on the TMI. "Ian understands that I need to try something new. He's not happy about it, but he accepts that it's what I need to do."

Abby groaned. "Why do you need to do it, Mom? I mean, really. Why are you leaving the job that you love?"

"I already explained why. I need a change."

"But *why*?"

Ella hadn't heard that many "whys" in a row from Abby's mouth in years. Her little girl had outgrown the "why" phase at the age of five. But now she sensed that her mom had held back a good portion of the story, and the "whys" wouldn't stop.

Having a smart, sensitive, perceptive daughter had a downside. Who knew?

Abby scowled. "Wait a minute. Is this Ian's fault?"

"It's my decision. Don't blame Ian. I mean that, Abigail."

"You didn't answer my question."

I got nothing. How pitiful is that? "Sometimes things just don't work out in life."

"What things?"

Ella knocked back a big gulp of ice water. "Eat your dinner. It's getting cold."

"Mom. What things?"

"That's all I want to say right now. I'm sorry if I'm disappointing you, but I have no more to tell you, except that everything will work out just fine. I've had a lot of offers from other companies over the years. I will reach out and get something new—interesting work that will pay the bills and challenge me. You and Ian will go on as always. He loves you very much and so do I, and that is never going to change." As those words left her lips, she recognized them as words parents might say to their children when they'd decided to divorce—and not amicably. This was nothing like the friendly, mutually agreed-upon divorce she and Philip had so carefully planned and executed nine years ago.

Ella and Ian had been so close—for so long now. Even closer than she and her first best friend, Philip. She'd honestly believed that nothing could ever destroy their friendship, that what they had was strong, deep and lasting. That they would always be there for each other no matter what, be each other's refuge, each other's sounding board, the one to count on, the one to call when it all went wrong.

She should never, ever have gotten into bed
with him.

Except, well…

No.

She couldn't bring herself to regret their weekend in Oregon. For a few beautiful days and nights,
they'd had it all, together.

She'd never had it all before.

At least now she could say she knew what it
meant to love a man completely, head to toe, inside out, heart and soul. She would hold on to that
now, when things felt so bleak and sad and empty.

"Oh, Mom…" Abby's big eyes looked misty,
and her shoulders had drooped.

"Sweetheart, don't be sad. Please. It's a good
thing. You'll see."

"Mom…" Abby got up and came to her.

Ella stood. They wrapped their arms around
each other. Tears burned behind Ella's eyes, too.
She blinked them back and held her daughter tight.
"I love you. So much," she whispered.

"Oh, Mom. I love you, too…"

Ella framed her daughter's face with cherishing
hands and smoothed her brown hair away from her
freckled cheeks. "So then. We're good?"

Abby nodded. "Yeah."

Ella nodded back. "Well, all right. We should
eat then, before it gets cold."

* * *

The Yankees played the Sox at two thirty that Saturday.

Ian used his car service to ferry him and Abby back and forth to Yankee Stadium. He picked her up at Philip's place, which worked out great—he didn't have to see Ella, didn't have to pretend for Abby's sake that nothing had changed.

Not that he had a clue what Ella might have told Abby. For a week now, he and Ella had only spoken when they needed to at work. He hated it— that she seemed to want nothing to do with him.

At the same time, he found himself waiting for her to come to her senses and realize that quitting the company would never really happen. He just knew she would come around and decide to stay on—aka, plan B, as he'd come to think of it. In plan B, she stayed at the company and slowly, over time, they worked their way back around to being best friends again.

As for plan A? He'd given up on plan A, in which they could continue as lovers until the hot thing between them wore itself out. He looked back on that now as his own deluded fantasy.

Wisely, Ella had nixed plan A right from the gate. He should have known she would never settle for that. Ella had it all going on. Someday she would get what she wanted with a very lucky man.

Not that he could stand to think of her with someone else. His jealousy of some guy she hadn't even met yet made him kind of want to punch himself in the face for being an idiot. He could have had a chance with her. All he had to do was ask for it.

But he'd already hurt her. If it didn't work out—which it most likely wouldn't, given all the ways he could possibly screw it up—she would only get hurt again. He couldn't bear to do that to her a second time.

And plan C? That was her plan, a very bad plan. The one where she left the company and their friendship ended for good.

Never going to happen. She would see the light about that eventually. And when she did, she would still have her job. Because he refused to start looking for her replacement. She didn't need replacing. Plan B would work out in the end. Ella wasn't going anywhere.

He glanced over at the cute kid in the back seat next to him. She had on her Yankees hat and her #45 jersey. "You're kind of quiet," he said—and then wished he hadn't. She might tell him why, and he might not like what she said.

But she only gave him a smile and replied, "Just thinking."

At least he had sense enough not to ask what. "Written any good books lately?"

That got her going. She started in about her latest literary creation. "I'm writing one now about a girl my age that nobody will listen to—well, it's not really that they don't listen. It's that when she talks, *she* can hear her words, but nobody else can."

"So at the end, do they finally hear her?"

Abby tipped her head to the side. Beneath the bill of her hat, he could see she wore a thoughtful frown. "Hmm. I'm not sure yet. Still working on that."

The floodgates seemed to open from there. She talked nonstop to the stadium and all the way to their seats. He listened to her voice, enjoyed her animated descriptions of things going on at school and the hip-hop class recital she expected him to attend in early June.

The game turned out to be a nail-biter, but the Yankees came through four to three.

Never once during the whole afternoon had she mentioned her mother. It bothered him a lot. He had Ella on the brain these days, and he should be grateful Abby didn't have a bunch of questions about her mother's decision to change jobs or…

Well, or whatever. No good could come of him and Abby discussing what might be going on with Ella.

It nagged at him the whole afternoon, though. How much did Abby know about him and Ella, about her leaving Patch&Pebble? He couldn't get answers from Abby without asking the questions. And asking the questions would most likely only end up making him wish he'd kept his damn mouth shut.

"Actually, Ian, we've been sitting all day," she said, so calm and thoughtful, like someone much older than eleven. "How about a walk? The High Line is nice, and it's close to my dad's."

He let the driver go, and they strolled the elevated paths of what used to be a freight rail line, ending up descending to a tree-shaded circle of benches around a pair of spray showers—two seal sculptures, one bright red, the other bold yellow. The seals sprayed mist to cool the air and give kids a little fun on a hot day. Abby dropped to a bench and patted the space beside her.

His butt had no sooner hit the seat than she turned to him, her freckled face sweetly serious, no dimples in sight. "I think we need to talk about my mom, Ian."

He gulped. Set up by a smart little eleven-year-old. He should have known this was coming. "Uh, sure. What's going on?"

Abby wore her patient look. She was like her mother that way, several steps ahead of him too much of the time. "I don't know, really. That's why I'm asking you. She loves her job, but she's quitting. Why?"

"Ah," he said, for lack of actual words as he mentally scrambled for the right thing to say to her.

"It just makes no sense to me, Ian."

"Well, what did she tell you?"

"That she's ready for a change and that you're not happy about her leaving but that you understand. What does that mean, Ian? What do you *understand*?"

The kid was too smart by half. And what the hell *did* Ella mean, anyway? He damn well did not *understand*. Not in the least.

Plus, he reminded himself, Ella would never leave Patch&Pebble, he felt sure of it. Plan B would win out. Just see if it didn't.

But however it went down in the end, Abby needed reassurance now. "Your mom is right. I don't know how I'll get along without her." That sounded good, didn't it? Plus, it was true. He *couldn't* get along without her, and he wouldn't have to when it all shook out.

Plan B. No doubt.

But he couldn't tell Abby about plan B, so he went with what her mother had told her. "It's your mom's choice. It's what she feels she needs right now. And no matter what happens, everything stays the same as far as you and me. You need me, you call me. I'll be at your hip-hop recital, down front and center. Nothing will change, Abby. I promise you that."

Abby still didn't show him even a hint of a dimple. Her big eyes remained way too serious, trained right on him. "That's not what I asked you, Ian. I asked you *why* my mom decided to quit her job suddenly?"

He stared in her eyes and felt hopeless. Hopeless and pissed off at everything in general. *Keep calm*, he ordered himself. *Don't lose it over this.* Abby needed comfort and reassurance, not his crap raining down on her.

But Abby's big brown eyes, expectant and trusting and frustrated, too—those eyes of hers combined with how much he missed her mother...

It all got to him.

It wrecked him.

His best friend had turned her back on him when he only wanted to protect her from his inability to be what she needed in a man.

He threw up both hands. "How the hell should I know? What can I say to you? It's what she wants. Ask *her*. *She's* the one who's leaving..." *Me.*

Somehow, he kept himself from saying that last, damning word. But not saying it didn't make it any less true. If Ella left, it would be him she was leaving.

Because she needed more than he knew how to give her. He had too many broken parts inside his heart. And he'd yet to figure out how to put them all back together. The broken parts kept him from getting on with his life in the important ways—like loving the right woman and starting a family.

The broken parts held him back from letting Ella know how much she mattered to him. He didn't want Ella to go. But she *would* go. And he was just blowing smoke up his own ass, pinning his hopes on plan B.

He needed to find a way to step up for Ella. If he didn't, plan C would happen. All his ridiculous denials to the contrary, she would go and stay gone. Forever.

At some point, it would be too late for them—for Ella and him. He needed to figure out how to pull it together before she left him behind.

Beside him, Abby seemed not the least bothered by his irrational outburst. Gently, she patted his hand. "It's okay, Ian. I'm not mad at you. But I would really like it if you would talk to my mom and make her feel better. Communication matters. It really, really does."

And from there, she launched into one of her stories about a book she'd just read wherein two smart young girls learned to open up to each other about what was bothering them.

"So that's what you need to do, Ian. Be honest and truthful, really *talk* with my mom."

What could he say to her? "It's good advice, Abby. Thank you."

"Don't just thank me. Do it."

When she looked up at him like that, with all the trust in the world shining in her eyes, what else could he say but "I will."

Sunday, Hailey called. A take-charge kind of woman, his sister got right to the point. "I'm putting the pressure on, Ian. My wedding is next Saturday. If at all possible, I want you there. We *all* want you there, all your brothers and sisters who have been missing you for twenty years. Will you please come?"

He opened his mouth to make excuses—and then realized he had nothing planned for next weekend. No mystery how things would end up if he stayed home. He would mope around his apartment, staring out the windows, thinking about Ella, feeling time slipping away from him. Every day, every hour, every freaking minute only brought him closer to losing forever what he wanted most but somehow couldn't let himself have.

Or maybe he'd already lost Ella completely and just hadn't allowed himself to admit it yet.

Whatever the reality of the situation, it sucked sitting home brooding about it.

"Ian. Did you just hang up on me?"

"I'm still here."

"Well? Will you come to my wedding, please?"

"Sure," he replied before he could think of all the reasons he had no interest in flying across the country for the wedding of a sister he barely knew.

A moment of silence, then, "Terrific. Everyone will be so happy to see you."

He couldn't help chuckling. "You're so determined."

"And damn proud of it, too. Bring Ella. And I want to meet Abby, so think about including her, too."

"Don't push your luck." He said it jokingly. But he wasn't kidding, not really.

"Fine. Just Ella, then."

"I'll see what I can do." Which would be nothing, but he didn't feel like going into all that, so he let his bossy little sister believe whatever she wanted to believe.

"Great. Did you get the invitation I sent?"

"Yes, I did."

"So you've got all the deets—and you know, there's plenty of room at our house for both you and Ella. Stay with us, why don't you? There's a whole separate suite, your own kitchen and separate entrance included, on the bottom floor." She lived with her fiancé, Roman Marek, and his toddler son, Theo.

"Thanks for the offer. I might take you up on it." No, he wouldn't. He needed his own space, and he didn't want to get down in the weeds with her about that.

"Just let me know—and I hope you can make the rehearsal dinner Friday evening…"

"I'll try." Would he? He just might. And that he might shocked the hell out of him. "And I got all the information you sent about that, too."

She stopped pushing, but she didn't say goodbye. For the next ten minutes, she provided updates on every little thing that had happened in Valentine Bay since he'd left two weeks before. He listened to her chatter and realized he kind of enjoyed listening to her. He might even kind of *miss* her—along with all his other siblings on the far side of the USA and their wives and husbands and cute little kids.

Yeah, Ella had predicted that would happen, that he would start to care for them, over time. He hadn't believed her. Plus, "over time" implied a long while, didn't it? It hadn't taken long at all.

Didn't matter, the whole caring thing. He'd decided to go. A weekend away would help keep his mind off Ella and her imminent departure from his company and his life.

He chartered a jet for the trip, a ridiculous extravagance for one person. But he could afford it. Nonstop flights at his convenience to and from the small airport just outside Valentine Bay made it all so much easier.

At three on Friday afternoon, he checked into his bare-bones room at a motel several blocks from the beach. The Isabel Inn and everywhere else in town had been booked for the weekend.

Didn't matter. A bed was a bed.

At five, he arrived at the old theater in the Valentine Bay Historic District where Hailey and Roman would say "I do." Hailey directed community productions in the theater. Roman had put his talents to work renovating the building, strictly adhering to its original structure and design. In the note Hailey had sent him along with the wedding and rehearsal invitations, she'd explained that the old theater had brought her and Roman together, so they'd decided to get married in it.

Half the family was already there. He got a lot of hugs and claps on the back just for showing up. They really did all seem glad to see him. And for the first time since Ella gave him her notice, he felt marginally less alone.

Both Hailey and Daniel asked after Ella. Ian said she couldn't make it. His brother and sister expressed regret at not seeing her and left it at that. He ended up sitting in the second row with a toddler in his lap—along with the others who weren't taking part in the ceremony.

After the brief rehearsal, they filed out into the lobby, where a catered dinner was served on white-clothed tables between the wide Tuscan pillars that held up the ceiling. He sat at a table with Matt, Liam and their families.

The speeches went on forever, mostly humorous ones about Hailey and Roman, who had both grown up in town, though Roman had moved away years ago. Last fall, he'd returned with his little son, Theo. Roman and Hailey had butted heads over the future of the theater. Sparks had started flying and hadn't stopped since.

Ian found he enjoyed the kids a lot—especially Liam's eight-year-old stepdaughter, Coco, who regaled him with stories of her performances in the *Festival of Fall Revue* and another big production titled *Christmas on Carmel Street.* "We put on the shows right here at the Valentine Bay Theater, Uncle Ian," Coco explained.

Next up would be the Medieval Faire, Coco

said. Hailey would be running that, too, this summer in a local park.

The evening kind of flew by. Ian thought about Ella constantly; good thoughts—how much she would have enjoyed this, his lost family, found at last. All of them together, celebrating Hailey and Roman and their new life as a married couple.

After the dinner, he let Daniel talk him into driving up to the Bravo house.

Surprise, surprise. His brothers drove up there, too. Daniel broke out the good scotch and the men sat on the big front porch in the mild late-May evening, sharing family stories until far into the night. Nobody asked him a single uncomfortable question. They let him be.

At two in the morning, having downed a couple more scotches than he should have, he accepted Daniel's offer of a bed for the night. He dropped right off to sleep in the downstairs bedroom off the kitchen, with the window to the backyard halfway open, letting in the cool night air and the smell of evergreens.

His dreams were vivid, real.

Good dreams. True dreams, because they were memories of his childhood in this very house. In those dreams, his past flooded back into him, filling the empty spaces in his mind. In his heart.

He'd given up this family once. There had

seemed no other choice at the time. He'd had to forget them, forget the past, in order to go on without them, to survive in a brutal land. But he woke on Saturday morning knowing he belonged to them again, as they to him.

He shared breakfast in the kitchen with Daniel, Keely, the four-and-a-half-year-old twins named Jake and Frannie, and the littlest one, Marie. Then he hung out with them, not returning to the motel until he needed to shower and change for the wedding.

At three that afternoon, Hailey married Roman on the stage at the theater that had brought them together. It was short and sweet and simple. Hailey, gorgeous in a white lace gown, had all her sisters for bridesmaids and her stepson, Theo, not quite two, as the ring bearer. Roman's mom, Sasha Marek Holland, kept the little one on track. Patrick Holland, the groom's stepfather, stood up as Roman's best man.

After the ceremony, horns honking, cans clattering behind Roman's Lamborghini, they caravanned out to Sweetheart Cove, where Liam and Madison and their families had side-by-side houses right on the beach. They'd put up party tents for the reception.

It was quite a party, too, with a big dance floor assembled not far from the shore and a six-piece band that played well into the night. When Madison and Sten urged Ian to stay over at their place, he didn't even argue, just stretched out on the guest room bed and dropped right off to sleep.

Sunday morning, Ian joined them all for a family breakfast at Madison's—Liam, Karin and their three kids, and Madison, Sten and their new baby, Evelyn Daffodil. Like yesterday up at Daniel's, Ian didn't want to leave.

And no one seemed to expect him to. He spent an hour shooting the breeze with Sten and Karin's dad, Otto. Later, he took a long walk on the beach with Madison, who said that she'd left acting behind and put her Bel Air mansion on the market. She and Sten and baby Evelyn would make their permanent home right here at Sweetheart Cove in Valentine Bay.

Matt showed up in the late afternoon. He said he was hoping Ian might stay over tomorrow, Memorial Day, maybe come on up to the farm on the outskirts of Astoria, where he lived with his wife and baby son.

Ian couldn't say yes fast enough. Matt followed him to the motel so he could check out and then led the way to the farm, where Ian shared dinner with Matt and his wife and the older couple who worked with them raising goats and sheep, fields of flowers, and produce they sold at farm stands, and to restaurants and local markets.

They stayed up late, just Ian and Matt in the company of Matt's sweet-natured, three-legged Siberian husky, Zoya, playing *Grand Theft Auto 5*, catching up on the past twenty years. An hour or so before they called it a night, Matt asked about Ella.

Ian told the truth. "She wants a real relationship. I'm not that guy."

"You might surprise yourself. With the right woman, anything's possible." Matt launched into the story of how he'd met Sabra seven years ago when she broke into his isolated cabin in Clatsop State Forest seeking shelter from a bad storm. "Took us four years to get on the same page at the same time. But in the end, here we are."

Ian said, "That's a great story."

Matt grinned. "And it has a moral, too. Never count love out. Eventually, you'll make it work." He fake-punched Ian on the shoulder. "Grab your controller, little brother. Let's play. I'm the mood to whup your ass."

Ian stayed until after dinner the next day. When Matt and Sabra walked him out to his rental car, they both urged him to come back soon. He found himself saying he would do that.

And meaning it, too.

His plane was waiting at Valentine Bay Executive Airport when he arrived. He slept through the flight, which took most of the night. At his loft, he left his suitcase in the foyer and went to the nearest window to watch the sunrise.

When daylight filled the space, he made himself coffee and breakfast. With a full stomach, he headed for the master bath to clean up.

At eight, he called Audrey to let her know he was taking the day off. "Can you clear my calendar?"

"Of course."

"Thanks, Audrey. You're a treasure."

"I certainly am. Jet-lagged?"

He wasn't, not really. He felt ready for anything. But he supposed jet lag would do for an excuse. "Yeah, I need the day."

She kept him on the phone for a while with the thousand and one problems she'd been saving up for him since Thursday. He listened, answered her questions, agreed with her solutions to all the issues she could solve herself and gave her instructions for everything else.

It was after nine when she finally let him go. He unpacked his suitcase, put everything away and called the car service. Fifteen minutes later, he ducked into the cool, dark interior of the town car.

And twenty-five minutes after that, he entered the Central Park Zoo.

Bypassing the tropic zone, he strode by the seals and the snow monkeys, headed straight for the bear habitat, where he found Betty and Veronica napping on the rocks.

He stood at the viewing screen in the gray light of the overcast day, staring at the two giant, oblivious bears, waiting for the panic to set in. It was a long wait.

And yet a strangely pleasant one. Women pushing strollers and a few random couples went by. More than one group of tourists observed the bears, each group with a guide to explain about Veronica and Betty and their individual journeys from the wild west to the Central Park Zoo.

The bears kept yawning, rolling over, making lazy growling noises, seeming completely satisfied not to do much more than lie there, easy and content in their giant, open-air cage.

Finally, one of them—Betty, he was fairly sure, the one with the blonder hair on her head—rolled into the stream below their resting spot on the rocks. She landed, then rolled again to get her giant paws under her. Sitting up in the water, she threw her head back and let out a mighty roar, displaying her long, sharp canines meant for ripping and those jagged rows of incisors that could cut to bits what the canines had ripped.

It should have happened right then, at the sight

of that wide-open mouth filled with so many flesh-tearing teeth. That should have triggered him.

But it didn't.

Betty shut her mouth and rolled to her back again. She wriggled a little, enjoying the water, and then set about climbing back up on the rocks.

Just a big, shaggy bear in the Central Park Zoo, lumbering about on the ledges well below him in the bear habitat, unable to reach him, no matter how hard she might have tried. Betty couldn't harm him—Veronica, either.

Just bears in the zoo.

And he was no longer a scared, lost little boy.

He knew where he came from and how he had gotten there. He knew who his people were—on both coasts. In the deepest sense, he belonged.

Belonged to the family of his early childhood, the family in Oregon who had never given up trying to find him. He belonged to Glynis, the mother who had found him, lost and unspeaking, alone in a strange land, the woman who had taken him home, healed him in every way she could, given him a good life. And when she died too soon and way too suddenly, she had left him prospering, with a bright future ahead.

But most of all, he belonged to Ella. And he had for years now, though he'd let his fears and his scars—the scars inside that no one could see—

keep him from knowing who she really was to him, keep him from admitting all that she meant. For too long, he'd let what had happened to him as a lost child hold him back.

Not anymore.

He needed to show her that he was finally ready for her—for all she had to give.

If only she hadn't turned her back on him for good.

If only she would give him one more chance…

Chapter Thirteen

Ella had schooled herself.

The lesson was simple: don't think about Ian.

Don't wonder where he went when his office remained empty all day Friday. Don't just happen to drop by Audrey's desk and ask her casually where the boss had gone.

All Friday, she kept herself from getting anywhere near Audrey. Even when Marisol had to back out on their usual Friday lunch and she ended up alone at her desk with takeout tom yum goong and Thai iced tea, Ella never let her weaker self take control.

But late Friday afternoon, she got her answer

anyway, when she heard her assistant, Samar, and Audrey chatting in the break room.

"Oregon, huh?" Samar asked.

"That's right. He's got family there, did you know?"

"I heard, yeah."

"One of his sisters is getting married this week-end…"

Although she had nothing to smile about where Ian was concerned, Ella felt a happy grin spread across her face. Hailey's wedding. He'd actually flown out there for it.

She should have guessed.

But she hadn't. He'd seemed absolutely deter-mined that he would never go back to Oregon, been so cold and confident about it that she'd begun to believe he meant what he said.

And yet, within a few weeks of that first visit, he'd flown back.

Ella wished she could've gone with him. She would have loved seeing Hailey get married in that old theater where she and Roman had met. Maybe she could have dropped by Wild River Ranch to visit Aislinn Bravo Winter's giant, fluffy rabbits, or maybe hung out with Keely, the twins and little Marie up at the Bravo house.

So sue her. Since it had all blown up in her face

with Ian, she'd let her envy of all he could have that he'd just turned his back on get to her a little.

Or maybe a lot.

Yeah, he'd had a rough go of it. But other people suffered, too, in life. Since ending it with Ian and giving her notice at work, she'd spent too many late nights after Abby went to bed sitting on the sofa in the dark, scowling at cable television and obsessing over the thousand and one ways Ian didn't appreciate all that he had.

At least he seemed to have finally seen the light that when you had a family like the Bravos, you didn't just go meet them and then never go near them again.

"Way to go, Ian," she muttered angrily under her breath, tiptoeing away from the break room so that neither Audrey nor Samar would know she'd eavesdropped on their conversation like some brokenhearted fool.

Which reminded her.

Clearly, she needed to get herself schooled all over again.

She needed to get over Ian once and for all.

And she was. She would.

Ian who?

Never heard of the guy.

In a week, she would leave Patch&Pebble for good. That would help. She would only ever have to see him again now and then if he happened to pick up Abby at her place. Mostly, Ian and Abby got together on the weekends, and most weekends Abby stayed at Philip's.

So big yay on that. As soon as she left the company, Ella might go for months without seeing his gorgeous face.

The long weekend crawled by, with Abby upstate. She'd gone camping with Philip, Chloe and the girls. Ella did some shopping. She cleaned the apartment and constantly reminded herself how she ought to dust off her résumé, update her LinkedIn profile and contact those headhunters. She tried not to wonder about Ian's trip to Oregon, not to picture all the smiling Bravos and Hailey in her wedding gown.

Philip dropped Abby off at six Monday night. Ella hugged her tight, breathed in her scent of insect repellent and dust—and felt better about everything, to have her daughter home again.

Tuesday morning, Ian remained absent from work. Had he stayed on in Oregon? Ella ached to know. But she made herself avoid the break room and keep well clear of Audrey's desk.

Marisol called her at eleven. "Charlotte's missing her bestie after the long weekend." Their tap class Monday had been canceled due to the holiday. "Okay with you if I have them over here at our place? They can hang out and have dinner, maybe even do a little studying. I can get her home by eight."

"Thanks. She'll love that."

"Good, then. We're set. And I've been missing you, too. Sorry I couldn't make our lunch Friday. It's been forever since we got together. Any chance you could steal an hour away today?"

They met at a Greek place they both liked.

Ella had taken just one bite of her gyro when Marisol said, "Charlotte reports that Abby told her that you quit Patch&Pebble."

"I did, yeah."

"You love that job, Ella."

She set down her sandwich. "I need to move on."

"Did you tell him how you feel?"

Ella tried not to wince. Okay, she hadn't, not exactly. But she didn't want to get into all that. Not now. "It's a long story. Can we save it for some future lunch, please—like, maybe a hundred years from now?"

Marisol stuck her fork upright in her salad, shoved back her chair and stalked around to Ella's side of the table. "Get up here." She grabbed Ella's hand and pulled her into her arms. "Hold on tight," Marisol commanded.

Sob-laughing, Ella hugged her friend good and hard.

"It's all going to work out," Marisol promised in her ear.

Ella didn't really believe her, but she agreed with her, anyway.

The rest of the day at the office? Four hours that took half a lifetime to go by. Nobody in the break room gossiped about Ian's current whereabouts, so she remained in the dark on that score.

At five o'clock she got out of there. Twenty minutes later, she let herself in her front door—and felt immediately at loose ends, with Abby at Charlotte's and a dinner alone to look forward to.

She'd just engaged the dead bolt and put the chain on the door when someone knocked on it. Probably one of her neighbors in the building.

But you never knew. Some creep could have slipped in downstairs behind her and followed her up. To be safe, she checked the peephole and got the shock of her life.

Ian?

Oh, God. She'd lost it. Now she was seeing him when no way he could be here.

She squinted through the tiny glass again.

Still Ian.

Her knees went to rubber. She turned, flopped back against the door and took slow breaths, waiting for...

What?

She had no idea.

He knocked again. "Ell, come on. I know you're in there. I followed you up."

That stiffened her spine. He had a nerve and a half, scaring her like that.

Whirling, she slid back the dead bolt, took off the chain and pulled the door open. "What are you doing here?" she demanded through clenched teeth.

He fell back a step. "I need to talk to you."

"Why?"

Cautiously, he tried to peer around her shoulder. "Is Abby here?"

"She's having dinner at Charlotte's."

"Good," he said quietly. "That's good. I was hoping to get a few minutes alone, you and me."

"What for?"

He just stood there, in perfectly tailored gray slacks and a crisp blue button-up, looking effortlessly hunky, with those thick, muscular shoulders and that jaw carved from granite beneath just the right dusting of scruff. "God," he said, sounding downright reverent. "You look good, Ell. I've missed looking at you." He stared at her so...longingly?

No. That couldn't be. Ian McNeill didn't *do* longing. "Ian?" she asked in a tiny voice.

"Yeah?"

"What's going on?"

He looked at her like he could just eat her right up. "Let me in? Please?"

She moved back and gestured him forward. He filled up her doorway and then he was inside, stepping past her, bringing his beloved scent of sandalwood and new-mown grass. She shut the door and indicated the far end of the hallway and the living area beyond.

He led the way. She followed numbly behind him, feeling strangely disembodied, like she'd landed in an alternate universe where nothing was as she knew it to be.

In the main room, she sucked in a shuddery breath and asked again, "What is it?"

"Ell. Damn it. I..."

She put up a hand. He fell silent.

They stared at each other some more.

And it came to her. This was her chance, to step up. To say it. To get it right out there, no matter what happened next, to override the lonely little orphaned girl inside her, to be strong and speak her truth out proudly. "Ian, I've been a coward."

"What?" He blinked and his head jerked back, like she'd slapped him in the face. And then he closed the few feet of distance between them and put his big hands on her, clasping her upper arms, holding her gaze, so sure and steady, those blue eyes full of heat and intention. "No, you're not.

No way. You're brave, Ell. The bravest, strongest person I know."

She lifted her right hand, brought it up between them and pressed her fingers to his warm lips, felt his breath flow down her palm. "I never said it. I need to say it." Her throat clutched and her eyes burned with hot moisture. But she didn't let the rising tears stop her. "I love you, Ian. I'm *in* love with you. I think I have been for at least four or five years now. I never even had a clue of it until that day in the hospital last month, when Lucinda said it right to my face. She said that everybody knew I was in love with you. She said I was pathetic."

His mouth had dropped open. "Say it again."

A smile trembled across her lips as she gently nudged his chin. "You're gaping."

"Damn straight. Say it again."

"That Lucinda said I was pathetic?"

He scowled. "Forget Lucinda. Just say it."

She sucked in a slow breath and told the truth. "I love you, Ian McNeill. I'm *in* love with you."

And he said, "That's good, Ell." His hands strayed upward, big, warm palms skating over her shoulders, up the sides of her throat until he framed her face.

She gazed into those unforgettable eyes of his and wished with all her heart never to have to look away. "Yeah?"

He nodded. "Yeah. I can't tell you *how* good. Because, Ella Ryan Haralson, I love you, too. So much. For such a long time, years of knowing you and not realizing what we had, what we were always meant to be. Tell me there's still a chance for me—for us. Tell me you haven't given up on me yet."

Her vision blurred. She had to blink the tears away. "I tried to give up on you."

He kissed her, a sweet brush of his mouth across hers. "I can't blame you. All these years. I've been such an ass."

"Yeah." She sniffled. "You *have* been an ass, so thickheaded. All wounded and unwilling."

"It took finding my family and thinking I had lost you to get me to open my eyes and see what's been right in front of me all this time—it's you, Ell. You're the one. You're *my* one. My only one…"

She could not survive another second without her mouth pressed to his. Surging up, she wrapped her arms around his neck and claimed his lips.

"Ell…" He groaned.

And then he kissed her.

And then, his mouth still locked to hers, he lifted her. She jumped up, wrapping her arms around him, sparing a second for gratefulness that she'd worn a flared skirt so she could wrap her legs around him, too. One of her shoes fell off and clattered to the floor. She kicked the other off to join it.

He held her tight, kissing her endlessly as he strode back down the hall to the first door, her bedroom. Carrying her in there, he turned and sat on the bed, still cradling her close in his lap, her ankles hooked behind his back.

The kiss continued, so deep, so hungry, for the longest time. She reveled in it, rocking against him, feeling how much he wanted her and wanting him right back, for now.

And forever…

Her mind could barely encompass the wonder of that—Ian and Ella, now and forever…

He caught her face in his hands again. "Look at me, Ell."

"Hmm?" She gazed up at him, her vision only slightly blurred by happy tears.

"This," he said, long fingers combing back into her hair. "Us. I'm talking forever, Ell. I'm talking you and me and Abby—maybe more kids if that's how it works out. I'm talking a lifetime. Could you do that, Ell? Would you take that chance with me?"

She pressed her palm to his lean cheek. "Funny you should ask. I was just thinking…"

"What? Say it. You're killing me here."

She laughed for sheer joy, pushed him back across the bed and got her legs folded under her, one on either side of him. Bracing her hands on the mattress, she got right down in his face. "I was just thinking that forever with you is what I want, what I've hardly dared to dream of."

"Ell..." He lifted his head off the mattress enough to kiss her again, a soft kiss, a kiss of promise, reverent and slow. "So that's a yes, then?" He growled the question against her lips.

"A yes, absolutely."

"I'll be yours, you'll be mine."

"As it should be, for today, for tomorrow, for all our lives." And she claimed his mouth with hers.

For a while, they didn't need words. They undressed each other and celebrated their union with more slow kisses, with long, lingering sighs and, ultimately, deep and mutual satisfaction.

In time, they got up. He put on his pants and she wore his shirt—and then they stood by the bed, looking at each other, barefoot, half-dressed with messy hair.

They both started laughing.

And he asked, "When, exactly, is Abby getting home?"

"Around eight."

He grabbed his flashy watch off the nightstand. "Forty-five minutes. I know she'll be happy, seeing us together..."

Ella snickered. "Yeah. But maybe we need *not* to look like we just crawled out of my bed."

He pulled her close and kissed her deeply. "Agreed."

So she gave him back his shirt and he put it on. She dressed in jeans and a knit top. They stood in her bathroom, side by side, combing their hair, grinning at each other in the mirror like a couple of naughty kids with delicious secrets no outsider could ever share.

And she thought, *This. A lifetime of this. Us, side by side, sharing the bathroom mirror. This is what it's all about, the dream I thought I would never get to live...*

But she'd conquered her fear and so had he. And that finally made it possible for them to reach for each other.

They ordered takeout. Once the delivery guy had come and gone, Ella locked up, but with the chain off so that Abby could let herself in. Over dumplings and Szechuan pork, Ian shared all the details of his recent trip to Oregon, including the rehearsal dinner, Hailey's wedding and reception, and his visits to the Bravo house, Sweetheart Cove and Berry Bog Farm.

"And you were right," he added. "I don't know how it happened, exactly, but I feel that I'm part of them now, one of the family."

"Because you are, very much so. We should go back again soon, take Abby this time."

"Gracie's getting married next," he said. "Soon. In a week and a half, to be exact. But we can make it. I'll charter a jet."

"Whoa. That's extravagant."

"What's money for except to spend on things you really want to do? And I've been thinking…"

"Tell me. Everything."

"It's just that there's something I failed to do."

She frowned at him. "Can't think what…"

He pushed back his chair. She gazed up at him, still puzzled.

But then he knelt at her side and took her hand. "Ella, I love you. You're everything to me. Will you make me the happiest man on earth and agree to marry me, to be my wife?"

"Ian…" Her eyes got all misty again. "Yes. Absolutely. I love you, too, and I can't wait to marry you." She bent and kissed him, taking her time about it, tasting Szechuan sauce and thinking that from now on, Chinese food would remind her of this perfect evening when she and Ian became so much more than just friends.

A moment later, as Ian sat back down in his chair and picked up his chopsticks, they heard Abby at the door, the key in the lock, the dead bolt sliding back, the sound of the door opening, shutting, the clinking of the locking process all over again.

And then Abby's rapid footsteps approaching down the hall. "Mom, I'm…" She stopped stock-still where the hallway opened into the living area. "Ian?" She shook her head, blinking, as though not quite believing what she saw.

And then, with a happy cry, she ran to him. He rose, opening his arms just in time for her to throw herself against him. Wrapping her arms around his waist, she squeezed good and tight.

When she looked up at him, she asked, "Are we all back together again?"

He stroked her straight brown hair, skated a finger down the bridge of her nose. "Yes, we are. Very much back together, more together than ever before." He glanced at Ella then, love and their future shining in his eyes.

"I knew it." With her arms still around him, Abby managed to jump up and down. "The minute I saw you guys just now, I knew that everything would be all right." She glanced over her shoulder and beamed at Ella. "You're keeping your job, right?"

Ian answered first, his gaze holding Ella's. "God, I hope so. I haven't hired anyone. I haven't even considered anyone. I just didn't want you to go."

Abby demanded, "Mom?"

Ella confessed, "I haven't been looking, either. Guess I'll just have to stay on at Patch&Pebble."

"I knew it!" crowed Abby. "You could never leave, and Ian couldn't let you go." She glanced up at him for confirmation.

"I can't speak for your mother," he said. "But you're right, Abby. I never want her to go."

"Then it's settled," declared Ella, rising, stepping closer to the two most important people in her world. "I'm staying." She and Ian gazed at each other, a long look, one that promised so much—all the days and nights to come.

Abby let go of Ian and pulled back a fraction. She eyed him and then Ella, and then she asked cautiously, "Are you guys…getting married?"

Ella nodded at Ian.

His smile got wider. "As a matter of fact, we are. Your mother has just agreed to be my wife."

Abby gasped. She stacked both hands on her chest. "My heart is beating so fast. You guys, I'm so happy." She hooked an arm around Ella and then one around Ian and side hugged them both, beaming up at them with a proud gleam in her eye. "You've been *communicating*, haven't you?"

"We have," Ian readily agreed. Ella felt a blush coming on from the way he looked at her. She knew he was thinking of the two of them, all wrapped up together in her bed, saying so much without uttering a word.

"A family, that's us." Abby's eyes shone so bright. She beamed up at Ian. "You're my second dad for real now. Just think about that."

"It's a good day," said Ian.

"The best day," agreed Ella, leaning toward him for a quick, sweet kiss.

Epilogue

The three of them—Ian, Ella and Abby—flew to Oregon ten days later for Gracie's wedding. Abby loved Valentine Bay and wanted to come back often. And they did come back, returning for two weeks that summer and then for five days during Abby's Christmas break.

Ella and Ian decided they wanted a place all their own to start their new life together. They bought a rooftop apartment in Chelsea, not far from Ella's co-op, which they sold, along with his loft in Tribeca. Their new place was large and full of light. Abby loved it, plus, she stayed close to her school and her dad, stepmom and little sisters, and her best friend Charlotte's apartment, too.

As for their wedding, Ella and Ian decided to get married in Oregon, on the Fourth of July of the following year. Ian chartered a jet and flew all their New York friends and family to Valentine Bay for the celebration.

He and Ella said their vows in the backyard up at the Bravo house. Ella had Abby for her maid of honor. Marisol, Chloe and Charlotte attended her, as well. Matt stood up as Ian's best man, with their three other brothers and Philip stepping up as groomsmen, too.

The reception took place on the beach under white canopies at Sweetheart Cove. Champagne flowed freely and they had music and dancing, the same as at Hailey's wedding the year before.

After dark, the town fireworks display lit up the sky out over the ocean. The band took a break for that. They all listened to the music broadcast by a local radio station to go with the pulsing lights high above. Sten, Madison's husband, had rigged up a couple of giant outdoor speakers and they blasted them out over the sand. Katy Perry sang "Firework" and the sky blazed bright with every color of the rainbow, the lights shooting high and falling to the ocean in a shower of sparks.

While everyone stared up at the bursts of fire high in the sky, Ian's bride took his hand and pressed it to her belly.

More than a little stunned, he stared into those fine dark eyes of hers, hardly daring to believe. "For real?" he asked gruffly. After all, he had everything. "A baby, too?"

She nodded, so beautiful in her filmy white dress, her hair down on her shoulders, tossed a little by the night wind the way he liked it best. "In early March, I think."

He pulled her close and wrapped his arms good and tight around her. They shared a slow kiss as more streams of light shot skyward.

"I never thought I would make it back," he said, still holding her close, his mouth a breath from hers. "Never thought I would find all I lost so long ago."

"But you did, Ian." She lifted enough to kiss him again, a quick kiss, sweet and true, a kiss of love, of belonging. "You found your way home."

"Home to you." His voice sounded ragged to his own ears, rough with all the big emotions, the ones that make a man ache in the best sort of way. "I love you, Ell."

"I love *you*. And I am so glad you made it home—to the family you thought you'd lost. And at last, to me."

* * * * *

*Watch for a whole new series
from* New York Times *bestselling author
Christine Rimmer,
coming in November 2021.*

*And for more romances about finding family,
check out these great stories:*

Making Room for the Rancher
by Christy Jeffries

The Night that Changed Everything
by Helen Lacey

Switched at Birth
by Christine Rimmer

Available now from Harlequin Special Edition!

WE HOPE YOU ENJOYED
THIS BOOK FROM

H HARLEQUIN
SPECIAL
EDITION

Believe in love. Overcome obstacles. Find happiness.

Relate to finding comfort and strength in the
support of loved ones and enjoy the journey
no matter what life throws your way.

6 NEW BOOKS AVAILABLE EVERY MONTH!

COMING NEXT MONTH FROM

⊕ HARLEQUIN

SPECIAL EDITION

#2839 COWBOY IN DISGUISE
The Fortunes of Texas: The Hotel Fortune • by Allison Leigh
Since she first met him months ago in Rambling Rose at the Hotel Fortune, Arabella Fortune has fantasized about sexy and sweet Jay Cross. Now she sets to find out how he'd intended to finish his last words to her: "I think you should know..."

#2840 THE BABY THAT BINDS THEM
Men of the West • by Stella Bagwell
Prudence Keyes and Luke Crawford agree—their relationship is just a fling, even though they keep crossing paths. But an unplanned pregnancy has them reevaluating what they want, even if their past experiences leave both of them a little too jaded to hope for a happily-ever-after.

#2841 STARTING OVER WITH THE SHERIFF
Rancho Esperanza • by Judy Duarte
When a woman who was falsely convicted of a crime she didn't commit finds herself romantically involved with a single-dad lawman, trust issues abound. Can they put aside their relationship fears and come together to create the family they've both always wanted?

#2842 REDEMPTION ON RIVERS RANCH
Sweet Briar Sweethearts • by Kathy Douglass
Gabriella Tucker needed to start over for herself and her kids, so she returned to Sweet Briar, where she'd spent happy summers. Her childhood friend Carson Rivers is still there. Together can they help each other overcome their painful pasts...and maybe find love on the way?

#2843 WINNING MR. CHARMING
Charming, Texas • by Heatherly Bell
Valerie Villanueva moved from Missouri to Charming, Texas, to take care of her sick grandmother. Working for her first love should be easy because she has every intention of going back to her teaching job at the end of summer. Until one wild contest changes everything...

#2844 IN THE KEY OF FAMILY
Home to Oak Hollow • by Makenna Lee
A homestay in Oak Hollow is Alexandra Roth's final excursion before settling in to her big-city career. Officer Luke Walker, her not-so-welcoming host, isn't sure about the "crunchy" music therapist. Yet his recently orphaned nephew with autism instantly grooves to the beat of Alex's drum. Together, this trio really strikes a chord. But is love enough to keep Alex from returning to her solo act?

HSECNM0521

*Since she first met him months ago in Rambling Rose
at the Hotel Fortune, Arabella Fortune has fantasized
about sexy and sweet Jay Cross. Now she sets to find out
how he'd intended to finish his last words to her:
"I think you should know..."*

Read on for a sneak peek at
Cowboy in Disguise,
the final book in
The Fortunes of Texas: The Hotel Fortune
by New York Times *bestselling author Allison Leigh!*

"I think you'd better kiss me," she murmured, and her cheeks turned rosy.

"Yeah?" His voice dropped also.

"If you don't, then I'll know this is just a dream."

"And if I do?"

She moistened her lips. "Then I'll know this is just a dream."

He smiled slightly. He brushed the silky end of her ponytail against her cheek and leaned closer. "Dream, Bella," he whispered, and slowly pressed his lips to hers.

He felt her quick inhale and his own quick rush. Tasted the brightness of lemonade, the sweetness of strawberry.

He slid his fingers from her ponytail to the back of her neck and urged her closer.

Her fingers splayed against his chest. She murmured something against his lips. He barely heard. His head was full of sound. Full of pulse beats and bells.

She murmured again. This time not against his lips.

He frowned, feeling entirely thwarted. "What?"

She pulled back yet another inch. Her fingertips pushed instead of urged closer. "Do you want to answer that?"

It made sense then. His cell phone was ringing.

Don't miss
Cowboy in Disguise *by Allison Leigh,*
available June 2021 wherever
Harlequin Special Edition books and ebooks are sold.

Harlequin.com

HSEEXP0521

Get 4 FREE REWARDS!

We'll send you 2 FREE Books plus 2 FREE Mystery Gifts.

Harlequin Special Edition books relate to finding comfort and strength in the support of loved ones and enjoying the journey no matter what life throws your way.

FREE Value Over **$20**

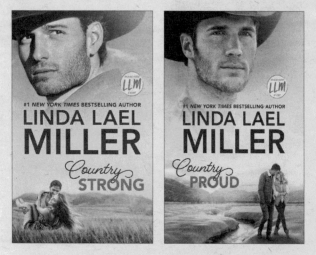